PSYCHOMANTEUM
Merita King

Published by Merita King

Cover art by Merita King Copyright 2014

OTHER WORKS BY MERITA KING

The Lilean Chronicles: Book One ~ Redemption
The Lilean Chronicles: Book Two ~ The Sleeping
The Lilean Chronicles: Book Three ~ Changing Faces
The Lilean Chronicles: Book Four ~ Avalanche Effect
Floxham Island ~ Sinclair V-Log AZ267/M
Bygora Vandos ~ Sinclair V-Log LB734/A
The Trials of Nahda ~ Sinclair V-Log PA884/R
Acts of Life
AWOL
Delectus Morbidium

ABOUT THE AUTHOR

I have loved the science fiction, fantasy, and horror genres in both books and movies since I was a young child. I have been greatly inspired by years of watching movies and reading books and have wanted to contribute to these genres for many years. I grew up watching science fiction and space opera television and movies, because those were what my parents enjoyed. My mother loved horror movies also, and we often used to watch the old black and white B movies and laugh our heads off. I can remember reading my mother's copies of the horror short story anthologies she collected, and being transfixed for hours by them. Throughout my childhood, I would get ideas for stories and plots but I did not have the ability or knowledge to write them down properly. The desire to write them never went away. I believe that the creative process is largely intuitive and can be effectively blocked by too much pre-planning. Plot lines, characters and events all come to me intuitively, and this makes the act of writing a constant pleasure. I live alone in Hampshire, UK.

1

The printer hummed into life, drawing the white sheets into its gaping mouth and vomiting them out the top, words littering the once pristine pages like the indecipherable remnants found on pavements outside the late night New York bars that kept Harlon awake at nights. He reached for them, glad to have gleaned some interesting snippets of this building's history from his five-hour internet search. Everyone knew that Gainsford House stood on what used to be Gainsford Hall, back in the days before New York was the sprawling metropolis it is now, but not many knew much about the old Hall's owner, Jonathan Rink-Standen.

The Rink-Standen family became prosperous due to Jonathan's timely decision to invest in a small local newspaper company. Under his guidance, and with his money behind it, the paper prospered and by 1900, was the most popular paper in the whole of New York. Jonathan seemed to have a good business instinct; he sold the paper at the height of its success for a fortune, and built Gainsford Hall on some of the proceeds. Once the sprawling mansion was finished and his wife and sickly baby daughter installed, Jonathan invested the remainder of his money into the production of printing presses, and he was responsible for several mechanical advancements that made newspaper printing and production, quicker and cheaper. He and his family enjoyed years of prosperity before the tide turned on them. October 1929 saw the Rink-Standen family's wealth disappear as the stock market crashed, heralding the start of the Great Depression.

Jonathan had enough money put away to see his family through those dark years, but by the time he reached his autumn years, he was forced to sell the Hall for a fraction of what it was worth. This unavoidable decision meant that the couple spent their last years in relative poverty. Leaving no children, their sickly daughter having succumbed to the flu epidemic of 1918, the Rink-Standen family died out when Emmalyn, Jonathan's wife, passed away four years after him.

Harlon poured himself another cup of coffee as he continued reading, skipping to where it told of the fate of Gainsford Hall. After being bought for a song, the Hall remained empty for seventeen years until the company who purchased it was itself bought out by a bigger company. Gainsford House, a twenty two-storey apartment block was built on the spot, the old Hall having been deemed too expensive to restore. The company believed that a city like New York needed to capitalise on what land was available. The priority at the time was housing as many as was possible whilst retaining a sense of luxury that residents could enjoy. Those who made such decisions at the time, decided that repairing the rambling mansion was too much of a waste of land.

"Well at least they kept the name," Harlon said to the empty kitchen. Pleased that he had been able to link the Rink-Standen name with his own family's history, he went back through to his office and perused his notes. Harlon Drake was enjoying researching his family tree, and was determined to find out more about his one successful ancestor, Patricia Drake. Living for twenty-eight years and four months before being found murdered in the grounds of Gainsford Hall, Patricia had enjoyed a measure of success as a watercolour artist. Several of her works still reside in two major New York galleries, and Harlon was proud of the connection. Luckily, Patricia had kept detailed records, and it was whilst trawling through the dusty sheets that he found out she gifted two of her paintings to Jonathan Rink-Standen at the height of his own success. Not much was known about the circumstances of Patricia's demise, other than the fact that Rink-Standen was not a suspect. She had been a friend of the Rink-Standen family, and a regular visitor to the mansion. On the night of her murder, there had been a party at the Hall, with thirty-seven people present, many of whom swore under oath that Jonathan Rink-Standen had been in their presence at the time of her murder. Several murders had taken place in the area during that summer, and Patricia's death was attributed to the unknown assailant.

What was left of Rink-Standen's effects passed to Emmalyn's relatives upon her death, and there the trail of the paintings went cold. Harlon had made extensive enquiries and found several surviving descendants, one of which remembered the paintings and knew where they were. Thomas Lorne, Attorney at Law, had inherited what remained of the Rink-Standen estate when his uncle, George Lorne, passed away childless. Thomas had stuffed everything away into storage and forgotten about it, concentrating at the time on his career. Several emails and a couple of phone calls had brought forth the news that Thomas Lorne, having just been divorced by his wife because of his infidelity and losing his home to her and their four children, needed to cut back on his expenses. The cost of the storage unit was too high for his current situation to bear, and he informed Harlon that he was auctioning the lot for whatever it would fetch. Determined to reclaim Patricia's paintings, Harlon decided to attend the auction and after investigating his own comfortable financial situation, decided he could spend up to eight thousand dollars without worry. The auction was the following day, and Harlon was both excited and nervous as he tossed and turned in bed, sleep evading him until well past two.

The auction room was packed and Harlon's heart sank when he read the brochure and saw that both of Patricia's paintings had reserves that were way beyond his means. Knowing he had no chance of securing them; he glanced through what else was on offer. It had taken him over two hours to get there, and he did not fancy leaving empty-handed. Nothing piqued his interest until the last page, when his gaze fell upon lot 851, a huge ornate ebony mirror and locked box of various books and documents. The mirror was ugly, so ugly it was beautiful, and Harlon knew it would fit right in with the decor and furnishings in his apartment, so he decided to bid for it. The box of books and documents was an unknown quantity and Harlon hoped that something within would prove interesting reading. There was no key for the solid metallic box, so what was contained within it was unknown. Its previous owner, Thomas Lorne, never got around to forcing it open due to his marital difficulties, and it remained unopened in his storage unit.

There was competition for lot 851, and Harlon found himself in a bidding war with an overweight woman whose gaze gave him the creeps. Another bidder, a thin elderly man lost his nerve at four thousand eight hundred dollars, and it was not until six thousand that the creepy woman gave in and shook her head as the auctioneer fixed her with his questioning gaze. Harlon was delighted at having won, but knew there was always the possibility that he had wasted his money on a turkey. He hoped the fact that the creepy woman bid so furiously against him, meant that lot 851 was worth having. The mirror was an outstanding piece and would look fantastic in his apartment, but was it worth six thousand? He did not think so but it saved him going home empty handed. He had a romantic notion that looking into the same mirror that Patricia might have looked into might form a connection between them.

PSYCHOMANTEUM

Harlon's apartment occupied a corner position on the twelfth floor of Gainsford House, his sitting room enjoying a dual aspect that looked out over the city. The large expanse of window gave the room plenty of light and a sense of space that went beyond its physical dimensions. The space between a matching pair of eighteenth century mahogany tallboys provided the perfect position for Harlon's new purchase, which reflected the already substantial light and lifted the slight heaviness it gave to the room. Standing over seven feet, the mirror was an imposing piece of furniture and it made Harlon a little uneasy when he caught his own reflection out of the corner of his eye. One night, three weeks after installing it, he came home late after a night out with some friends, and found the unlit sitting room looking decidedly spooky reflected in that mirror. Harlon laughed and thought it fitting that such a spooky piece should reside within this building, given the rumours.

During his research into the history of the building in which he had made his home, Harlon discovered many tales of paranormal activity, dating back to the time of the building's construction. A stonemason had been terrified out of his wits by a ghostly apparition, and had refused to return to his job, even preferring to leave his tools behind on the site than return there to collect them. Several other workers told of seeing the spectre of a fat man lumbering along the ground floor corridor, which disappeared right through a wall. Harlon found these tales fascinating, given that he was something of a believer in ghosts, and did some more research into these tales. He found that several murders occurred during the time the Rink-Standens occupied Gainsford Hall, one of which was his own ancestor Patricia. Not long after Patricia's murder, the killing spree stopped and there were rumours and talk of ghosts and several reports of people apparently being possessed by spirits and made to do unspeakable acts. The police at the time had not taken it at all seriously, and put the rumours down to too much hard liquor and not enough hard work. Harlon laughed as he read the reports. What 'unspeakable acts' might they be?

A few of the building's current residents accepted that Gainsford House was haunted, and Harlon could not bring himself to dismiss this belief. He had experienced some weird things himself since moving in, and although he had not seen a solid manifestation of anything otherworldly, there had been moments when he would swear blind he was not alone in his home. The most frightening experience was when he was watching the television late one evening seven months after moving in. The talk show had finished when the

4

door to the sitting room swung slowly and silently open. Harlon noticed the movement out of the corner of his eye, and his heart leapt in his breast as he watched the door open right back to the wall, where it sat for a few seconds before suddenly slamming shut with a bang that shook the pictures that hung upon the wall. The next time he met old Mrs Hanny in the corridor, he mentioned it and she told him that she had experienced something odd that same night.

Although not a religious man, Harlon decided to get the apartment blessed after that, and nothing similar had happened since. Mrs Hanny had sniffed at his decision to have a priest "with all his mutterings" visit, and declared that "there be evil around 'ere, Mr Drake, and no amount of Latin ramblings and wafting smoke is gonna change it. Something ain't right here, you mark my words, lad." Harlon thought Mrs Hanny was a little too firm in her belief of all things otherworldly, and decided that she had far too strong a conviction in the existence of evil. He laughed to himself as he thought of her, muttering her prayers and wafting her hands to 'feel the energies' whenever the subject came up between them.

"What a kook," he grinned as he washed the dishes after his evening meal.

Harlon had tried unsuccessfully on several occasions to facilitate communication between himself and the spirit of Patricia Drake, and had visited mediums in the hope of learning of her existence on some other plane. She fascinated him, and he admired her greatly for having been a successful single woman in a time when such an existence would have made her an oddity. Her life being cut short so early, and in such a dreadful way served only to make her more of a mystical and wonderful figure, and had been the sole reason Harlon had bought the apartment and set up home in Gainsford House. The fact that she died in the grounds of the old mansion that once stood on the spot made him think about her spirit. Would she now be haunting Gainsford House? The possibility was all the encouragement he needed so he bought an apartment.

It was three weeks after installing the mirror in his apartment that Harlon remembered the locked box of books. With deadlines at work bearing down on him, meetings to set up and a big contract to fulfil, he had stuffed them in the back of his hall closet and forgotten them. Now things had settled down he remembered them. He padded through to the closet and drew the box out from under the basket of scarves and gloves, swearing under his breath as he stubbed his toe on the edge of the doorframe. The box in his arms, he staggered back through to the sitting room, set it down on the floor and searched for something with which to break open the lock. A few blows with a hammer and a carefully placed screwdriver later, he settled himself on the sofa to go through the contents.

"Okay, Jonathan, what have you got for me huh?" he said as he reached in and grabbed the nearest book. First came a fat and far too well thumbed dictionary, followed by three encyclopaedias. With a growing sense of dread, he reached into the box again and noticed a few more books at the bottom. He lifted out the first. It turned out to be a first edition copy of A Tale of Two Cities by Charles Dickens, and Harlon gaped. This volume was probably worth a considerable sum of money.

"Wow," he hissed as he carefully examined it. "If there are any more like this one, I might just get my money back. Thanks, man." The next few volumes turned out to be more first editions. There was a mint condition Adventures of Tom Sawyer, which almost sent Harlon into a breathless panic attack. Not only would this volume alone allow him to recoup his outlay, but provide much more besides. A signed first edition Gulliver's Travels followed, along with a first edition copy of The Life of Samuel Johnson. Harlon gaped afresh as he lifted each new treasure from the dusty metal box.

"Holy shit, look at this," he gasped as he gently caressed a first edition War of The Worlds. "I loved this movie." He gently laid it down next to the other treasures and reached into the box again, almost afraid of what he might find. A single book lay at the bottom of the box, its plain leather cover curling up at the edges and showing that whatever this book was, it was well used. Harlon gently lifted it from the box and examined it, to find neither title nor author inscribed upon the black leather binding. It was a thick book, and by the state of the page edges as they lay between the front and back covers, Harlon guessed that however much it was worth, the state of it would probably decrease its value. He opened the cover and found a simple handwritten note.

Personal Journal of Jonathan Rink-Standen. Observations and experiences from the Psychomanteum.'

"My god, his diary. Psychomanteum? What the hell is a Psychomanteum?" he asked as he turned the page and began to read, and in so doing, set himself upon a path from which he would soon be powerless to return. A path upon which he would open the door to a horror the like of which he could never dream during his worst nightmares. A path which, once that first step was taken would draw him inexorably towards destruction. Harlon dragged himself to bed at four twenty in the morning, his body aching with fatigue but his mind racing as he tried to make sense of what he had read. Sleep finally embraced him after an hour of tossing and turning. When he woke well after mid-day, his mind was made up. The decision having been made, the clock began counting down.

PSYCHOMANTEUM

2

Harlon shrugged apologetically as the man hefted the heavy bags into the back of his truck.

"You moving or something?" he asked.

"No, just clearing out some junk I don't need," Harlon replied. "I've become a bit of a hoarder."

The man sniffed. "Well this junk will come in mighty handy at the homeless shelter."

"Great. Thank you for taking it all."

"No problem. Thanks for donating. Give us a call if you have any more junk."

"I will." Harlon waved as the truck pulled away, black smoke belching from the exhaust. With an excited clap of his hands, he raced back up to his apartment and examined the now empty hall closet. He had been ruthless with himself when deciding what to keep and what to get rid of, and the few essentials were now deposited in various other closets and hiding places around his home. He stepped inside the closet and was pleased to see that it was a lot bigger than it appeared when full of his possessions. There was enough room, he decided. While the motivation was hot, he went to fetch some cleaning materials. An hour and a half later, the closet was vacuumed, washed, cleared of cobwebs and Harlon was opening a paint can. By the time he stepped out of the shower, shortly before midnight, the whole apartment smelled of the matte mustard yellow paint. After opening the windows to let out the fumes, he dragged himself to bed and slept better than he had in weeks.

The next day, after a hearty breakfast, Harlon faced his biggest challenge - getting the huge ebony mirror from the sitting room, into the newly decorated closet. A trip down to the maintenance room in the basement of Gainsford House, and a few dollars to George, Gainsford's maintenance man, got Harlon the use of a two-wheeled dolly truck with which he moved the mirror without injury to himself. He sat down with some fresh coffee and re-read Rink-Standen's journal. Jonathan Rink-Standen had, it became clear as Harlon read the journal, nursed a secret obsession for everything mystical, and had pursued spirit communication with gusto at every opportunity. Séances, spells, incantations, meditations, all had been investigated at the Gainsford mansion but none had given Rink-Standen the results he sought. Then he had read some old paper about the setting up and use of a Psychomanteum, and with his natural desire to experiment driving him forwards, he set up his own in one of the basement rooms of the mansion.

Harlon had never heard of a Psychomanteum before, so he set about doing a bit of research on the internet, and was delighted to learn that it was a method by which one can 'see through the veil' as Rink-Standen put it in his journal, and hopefully communicate with those in the spiritual realm. In theory it seemed simple; a windowless room with low light and bland decor, a comfortable chair in which to relax, and a mirror in which to gaze. The whole set up designed so that one's eyes cannot focus on anything, and with a calm state of relaxation, the spiritual realm might be glimpsed within the mirror. Harlon knew about meditation, he had learned about it during his first attempts at securing communication with the spirit of Patricia Drake, and although he had not succeeded in his quest, he found the practice beneficial to his general state of mind, and had continued with it ever since.

Jonathan Rink-Standen described his Psychomanteum in detail in the journal, and Harlon wanted to copy it as closely as he could, although his closet was smaller than the basement room Rink-Standen had used. He was excited to know that he was to be using the same mirror that Jonathan had used for his own experiments, which had proved successful, according to his entries in the journal. It seemed that Rink-Standen had experimented with both a low light, and flickering candle light, and both had gleaned an equal measure of success, but Harlon decided that a low light bulb would be safer in the confined space of the closet. He had no desire to set fire to the building, so he purchased a small lamp with a domed glass shade that enclosed the bulb. After painting the shade with some of the same paint he used on the walls, and the lowest power bulb he found, he was pleased with the result and decided he was ready to try it. He read Jonathan's entry detailing his own first attempt.

"I sat back, and admit now to feeling a little anxious about what might transpire. After a few minutes, I allowed my mind to relax and my gaze to settle into the mirror. The effect was immediate, and my peripheral vision soon began to fade as my eyes got used to having no stimuli upon which to settle. Being used to the daily practice of meditative techniques, I cleared my mind and tried to maintain an open and accepting attitude. After what seemed to be no more than two or three minutes of gazing, I became aware of a thin

smoke begin to make itself apparent. This continued for what seemed like several minutes and then stopped without returning, despite my remaining in the aforementioned fashion for several more minutes. I ended the experiment for the night and am pleased to have had something of a result so quickly."

"Okay, smoke," Harlon said, closing the journal. "That'll be cool to start with." He closed the closet door and sat down, a little nervous now that the moment to begin had finally arrived. He reminded himself that Patricia Drake was a nice woman and not something he needed to be afraid of, took a deep breath, and relaxed. He allowed his gaze to settle into the middle of the mirror and calmed his mind, breathing deeply and rhythmically as he did during his regular meditation practice. Although not as disciplined as Jonathan Rink-Standen, Harlon kept to the practice three times a week and found himself deeply relaxed within a few minutes. His eyes found it difficult to settle at first, not having anything on which to focus, but once he got the knack of letting his gaze soften, it was easier. After what seemed like five minutes or so, he noticed shadows playing in the mirror. At first feint, they gently undulated as they faded in and out and Harlon had to force himself not to try to focus on them, as when he did, they disappeared immediately. Once he let his eyes rest without following them, the shadows strengthened, flowing across the surface of the mirror like a gently rolling tide, and at one point, covering the entire surface before flowing away and disappearing.

Harlon awoke, the pain in his neck making him grimace, and sat up.

"Dammit." He cursed aloud at the knowledge that he had fallen asleep during his experiment. Glancing at his watch, he was shocked to discover it was three in the morning. He had sat down at half past nine the evening before and been asleep in the chair for most of the night. From what he remembered, he guessed he had been awake for about an hour before falling asleep. His neck was stiff and painful from lolling to one side as he sat in the chair, and he grimaced as he rolled his head around. Jonathan Rink-Standen had not fallen asleep, at least his journal did not record it if he had, and Harlon was disappointed. With a yawn, he got up, stretched, and went to the bathroom before making himself some hot chocolate and going to bed.

Harlon did not greet seven o'clock with warmth. After a broken night's sleep and with a full day of meetings ahead, he groaned as he dragged himself from his bed. He hoped one of the meetings would result in the company securing a major contract that could net him a sizeable bonus at the end of the year, so he made the effort to get up and out on time. The day dragged by, and despite the meetings ending successfully, Harlon's mind was filled with his new obsession, and his hopes that it would finally help him to communicate with Patricia Drake. He was eager to get home and was so absorbed by his thoughts that he almost missed his bus stop.

The police officer looked up as Harlon entered Gainsford House, swept him up and down with his eyes, then looked away and continued his conversation with the concierge. It had been a while since Harlon had seen a police officer in the building. What was he doing here? Old Doug Morrison was waiting at the elevator, his almost sightless eyes examining him as he approached.

"Howdy, Mr Drake. Finished for the day?"

"Hello, Doug, yes. How are you these days?"

"Fine. At least I was until last night. Had an intruder. Almost peed myself when I saw him standing right in the middle of my kitchen as bold as you please."

"An intruder? Holy shit, are you okay?"

"Oh I'm fine. I might have been scared out of my wits for a second or two, but I ain't nobody's pushover. I'm eighty-two years old next month, and I've seen things that would unsettle any man. I served my country and took a few lives when I had to, and I'm more than happy to defend my life and property now. I may be almost blind but I ain't feeble y'know."

"I can believe it," Harlon replied, smiling at the old man's nerve. "So you chased him off?"

"I surely did. I raised Bessy here," he said as he patted his walking cane, "and yelled ma head off so loud that Rosy Newland came running down from number thirty two. The sound carries y'know, through the air conditioning vents."

"Good for you. Is that why the cop is here?"

"Yeah. Had to make a statement and give a description. Ha, a description, me."

"What could you tell him?"

"Not much, other than he was as wide as he was tall, wore a coat made out of animal hair, and he hadn't bathed in at least a month."

"How did you know his coat was animal hair," Harlon frowned.

"The smell. Wet animal hair smells distinctly. My eyes ain't no good any more, but my nose is as sharp as ever."

"Oh yeah. I've heard that when folks lose their sight, their other senses take over."

"Damn right," Doug nodded. "I can smell a rat fart in a sewer, and I swear that coat was animal hair."

"I hope they find him."

"So do I. The cops gave me this personal alarm thing. Told me to use it if he comes back. So if you get woken up in the middle of the night by an air raid siren, head up to my apartment with your gun."

"I don't own a gun."

"Got a baseball bat?"

"Yeah."

"That'll do."

"I'll remember. Well this is my floor. Take care, Doug."

The news an unwelcome visitor had preyed upon Gainsford House and a vulnerable elderly man had his home invaded made Harlon pay attention to his security more than he usually would. He decided to get a couple of extra locks for his front door, and momentarily entertained the idea of getting a dog, but quickly dismissed it when he remembered it would need walking every day. One of his work colleagues told him how he had set up his own closed circuit television for his home, and Harlon thought it a good idea to ask his advice on getting one for his apartment. Embarrassment flushed his cheeks at the knowledge that he was being far less brave than old Doug probably had been. Harlon always exchanged pleasantries with Doug whenever they met, which was usually at the elevator, but their conversations had never touched upon anything remotely personal. He was surprised that the old man he knew as an almost blind and vulnerable average old person, had been in the military, and then he cursed himself for forgetting that old Doug, was young Doug once. The aroma of freshly brewing coffee filled the apartment as he remembered what the old man had told him about himself. He said he had taken lives when he had to. Would he be able to take a life himself if the need arose? With every ounce of his being, Harlon hoped he never had to find out.

Images of old Doug, wearing nothing but his underwear, yelling at the top of his voice and waving his stick in the air, made Harlon laugh aloud, the sound echoing around the kitchen. More laughter ensued when another image, this time of Rosy Newland, hair in curlers and wearing something with several layers of bright pink chiffon, rushing downstairs to find Doug in his underwear. Harlon could almost see her hand go to her mouth in shock, the startled cry, and he slapped the counter top as he laughed. Once he stopped laughing, he thought perhaps the decent thing to do, would be to give Doug his phone number, in case he needed someone in the night. Although not sure how much protection he had the ability to give, Harlon guessed that the old man would be happier having another man to call upon, rather than Rosy Newland from number thirty-two in her pink chiffon.

Doug Morrison answered the door at Harlon's second knock, and peered through the narrow gap afforded by the security chain.

"Who is it and what do you want?"

"It's me, Doug, Harlon Drake."

"Oh howdy, Mr Drake, c'mon in." The door closed and Harlon listened as the old man fumbled with the chain, before opening the door and standing aside. "What can I do for you?"

"I hope you don't mind, but I want to give you this." He handed over the slip of paper with his phone number on, written in large letters so the old man could read it. "Just in case anything else happens and you need someone to come see you're okay. I can't guarantee I'll be much more help than Rosy Newland, but I do have that baseball bat I told you about."

"Well that's mighty thoughtful of you, thank you."

"You're welcome, Doug, and don't hesitate to call if anything worries you. I can be here in less than a minute."

"I must admit it was kind of awkward standing there in my underwear with Rosy Newland looking at me."

Harlon laughed. "I'll bet it was. How did she get in anyway?"

"She has a key. She offered to check in on me from time to time, so I gave her a spare."

"Did you mention that to the cops?"

"Yeah, they asked about it so I told 'em the truth. They checked the cameras in the hallway, and saw her come down at the right time. It couldn't have been her anyway, there's no way you could fail to recognise her in all that pink fluff."

Both men laughed, and Harlon nodded. "True, but it's not impossible that she could have had a copy made and given it to someone. Do you have any valuables that she knows about?"

"You should've been a cop, Mr Drake. They asked me that too, and whether she has any male visitors I know about, have we ever argued, and all sorts of other stuff."

"Good. At least they're doing their job properly. Remember, call if you need to okay?"

PSYCHOMANTEUM

3

In the years since the portal closed, It had slumbered. Time was of no consequence and because of this, It was unable to be irritated by the slow passing of the years. All It knew was that the portal had closed, necessitating a period of waiting until it opened again. Wars came and went, economies faltered, and life went on, unnoticed by the slumbering beast close by. Life was Its antithesis, Its counter, and Its opposite. It could wait for millennia if necessary, without impatience or awareness of the passage of time. It slept on, and waited.

It woke, and knew instantly that the portal was opening again, the fetid odour of life energy the distasteful but only key capable of opening it. This Portal Keeper was inexperienced, and would not be capable of opening it for long, if at all this first time. Vague memories of a previous journey through this same portal filtered through, and It remembered the last keeper to open it. That one was inexperienced too, but strong and determined, and it was that strength that enabled him to close the portal once he knew what was coming through. Anger and hatred flooded through what resembled Its mind at the memory, and it was glad that this one did not possess such strength.

Blinding light pierced the comforting darkness, and It instinctively drew back in fear. With the light came the overpowering stench of life, the urgent thrumming of millions of life energies almost painful. It knew the only place to find its own sustenance was within that stinking noisy hell. Summoning all of its strength, It approached the portal and sent a tendril of energy through, probing for the Portal Keeper's own energy. When he was safely asleep, It flung the portal wide and flew into the light, the stink of life almost too much to bear. Noise and stench came from everywhere, blood rushing through living flesh, thoughts clamouring inside empty minds, beating hearts, bodily excretions and the foulest thing of all, the love of life.

It raced into the hell, fighting the urge to retreat, and searched for sustenance. It raced along corridors, flew through walls, fleeing when the stench of a couple having sex became too much to bear. The urge to create more life, the hellish clamour of the desire for life was everything It was not. It wanted one thing and as it came to a halt in a darkened kitchen, It found what it needed. The old man still carried the fetid odour of life, but the heart beating inside that carcass of flesh was tired, slowing, and the mind did not cling so heartily to what thread of existence it was still able. This one knew that its end was near, but did not fear it. He merely waited for it. Knowing that the indistinct but unmistakeable shape of a human form within one's own personal space would bring forth a stronger surge of fear than would an amorphous dark misty form, It forced itself into the shape of a human. Before It could consume the delicious soul it smelled within, the old man opened his mouth and yelled at the top of his voice and waved a stick. It was aware of other energies nearby that had heard the cries and if they came to investigate the noise, the stink of the living would be overwhelming. This was too much for it to bear whilst weak from years of waiting, so it flew from the building and out into the night.

As It re-entered the portal and allowed the Portal Keeper to awaken, a block away, a call was being made to the police. The officers arrived and saw the bodies, realised they were beyond help, and called in the team.

4

After falling asleep during his first attempt in his Psychomanteum the previous evening, Harlon decided to schedule his sitting earlier in the evening. After a coffee and a light snack to satisfy his immediate hunger, and so his stomach would not make noises while he was trying to meditate, he went to shower and change. The hot water revived him, and he thought of Patricia Drake, and what he would say to her if he ever did get the chance to communicate. The main thing he wanted her to know was that he admired her greatly, and the courage she had shown by being a single woman earning her own living in days when that simply was not done by nice ladies, inspired him on a daily basis. He wanted to know how she had died, and who had taken her life so cruelly, and if she was happy wherever she was.

Harlon was aware first of the light, which although almost non-existent, seemed to darken a little more. He had been sitting for several minutes, and was reaching a point of deep relaxation when the shadows cast by the light lengthened and seemed to close in further around him. He was delighted that something was happening, and kept his gaze on the mirror. As he gazed, pools of shadow undulated and poured slowly down, around, and up again in a continuous lazy flow. It appeared to Harlon that the surface of the mirror itself was changing, becoming fluid, and that he could if he wished, put his hand right through into some other dimension. The slowly churning shadows gradually gained solidity under Harlon's continued gaze, and as they did so, they seemed to move away from the surface of the mirror and explore the empty air within the tiny closet. Such was Harlon's amazement at what was happening that his hold on his meditative state slipped a little, causing the shadows to recede and the mirror to return to normal. In desperation, he tried to relax and calm his excitement, and for a moment, the shadows returned long enough for a tendril of shadow to reach toward him.

Harlon drew back in fear, instantly alert and gasped deep breaths as he regained his senses. Leaping up from the chair, he opened the door and ran out, not bothering to switch off the light behind him. Leaning on the wall for support, his chest heaved as his heart thumped and the adrenaline coursed through his body.

"Jesus. What the fuck was that?"

Over dinner, he read more of Jonathan Rink-Standen's journal, and found that he had experienced similar results in the early days of his experiment, although he continued to write about seeing a milky coloured smoky haze and not shadows.

"I guess everyone will have slightly different experiences," he reasoned, remembering the time when he first investigated meditation. The books and articles he read at the time all seemed to give the impression that no two people will report identical experiences, so he relaxed and cursed himself for his fearful outburst. Perhaps it was Patricia Drake reaching out, he thought. Maybe she was around and so delighted that he was trying to communicate that she rushed forwards at the first opportunity.

"Damn." Suddenly remembering that he had left the light on in the closet, he got up and went along the hall to the still open door.

"I'm sorry for being scared," he whispered to the empty room despite feeling silly doing it. If Patricia was still around, he wanted her to forgive him and to try again next time. "Next time huh?"

Three floors above Harlon, Nessy Bellinger awoke and swore at the TV. The talk show had finished and she had missed the interview with her favourite actor.

"Shit." She straightened up and rolled her neck around, wincing as the knots complained. Reaching for the glass on the side table, she cursed when she found it empty, hauled herself from the chair and headed for the kitchen. Two steps along the hallway something pricked inside her mind and was instantly alert, her awareness switching ever so slightly as she listened within. At first, she heard nothing, but then the familiar energy of the female spirit enveloped her and she relaxed. This time she did not speak but brought forth images, thousands of them all tumbling and spinning around and through each other, so fast that Nessy could not keep up with them.

"Please, slow down. You know I can't understand you unless you slow it down a little. I'm still in a physical body; I can't work as quickly as you."

The racing images slowed and Nessy concentrated. What she saw sickened her and her hand went to her mouth as her mind registered blood-spattered walls, bodies hacked to pieces, and ransacked rooms. Then the sounds came, the screaming of women, the begging of an old man for his life, a baby's cry cut off far too suddenly, wailing police sirens, and then another sound. This cry, no, exultation, was not of this earth, of that Nessy was sure immediately. This was something else, inhuman, and its cry was one of blood lust satisfied. The last image she saw before she ran to her bathroom to vomit was out of place amongst the gore fest she had been witness to. The ugly but beautiful dark framed mirror seemed benign, but Nessy knew that it was inextricably linked to everything she had seen. She breathed hard, trying to calm her heart as it thumped in her breast, and knew with every fibre of her being that something awful was going to happen. She also knew that she, the quiet single woman whom no one ever noticed, was to have a central role within whatever was to come. The female spirit would not have shown her the images otherwise.

Nessy Bellinger was four years old when her parents noticed that she seemed to know things before they happened. One night, as her mother tucked her into bed and read her a story, young Nessy insisted that her Uncle Joe was in the room, covered in blood and with a knife in his chest. Molly Bellinger laughed away her daughter's imaginings, worried as to where she got such awful imagery. She took a lot more notice the next morning though, when her sister in law telephoned in tears to say Joe had died the night before after being stabbed outside a bar. Over the years, young Nessy told them about seven deaths, family members and close friends, and helped her parents avoid a nasty accident by insisting they change their road trip plans one weekend.

When Nessy grew up, she found close proximity to people overloaded her senses and made her extremely uncomfortable. Their worries, fears and more importantly, their deceased relatives, all clamouring for her to communicate their survival to their loved ones. Finding a career that enabled her to make a decent living whilst avoiding contact with too many people limited her options. She eventually settled on a career as a Librarian and found the enforced quiet was of great benefit in calming down the onslaught. Nessy found that when people were reading, their minds would switch into a different wavelength, their psychic needs temporarily stilled. With her parents' death had come a small legacy, enough to allow her to buy an apartment in Gainsford House and live in modest comfort. She had been in her new home for ten days when the female spirit first made her presence known, and over the intervening eight years, they built a strong bond of friendship and trust. When Patty told her that something was going to happen, it happened, and Nessy would not contemplate believing that today was to be different.

PSYCHOMANTEUM

Harlon had got over his fear by the time he climbed into bed, and decided to forge ahead with his experiment and learn to control his fear. After all, fear of the unknown is a natural human instinct, he reasoned. He would discipline himself to resist the urge to succumb to it next time it happened. He drifted off to sleep, firm in the belief that the dead are people, like us but without their bodies. There is no reason to fear the dead, he declared to himself, there is nothing to fear from reaching through the veil.

The following day, Harlon made enquiries about selling the first editions from the Rink-Standen collection, and secured an appointment with a well-respected firm in Albany. He set out after work, having booked a hotel room and arrived in Albany three and a half hours later, tired and hungry, but glad to see some new surroundings. The hotel food was plain but enjoyable and the view from his fourth floor window, pretty. At ten o'clock the next morning, Harlon handed over the books for Frances Durrell to peruse, and was delighted to see his eyebrows shoot up as he examined each one. Fifty minutes later, he emerged from the smart office building and headed for the bank. He had no desire to carry such a large cheque around with him any longer than was necessary, so he paid it into his account straight away. The teller did a double take when he handed it over, and he almost laughed aloud at her incredulity.

"Wow did you win the lottery or something, Mr Drake?"

"No, Ma'am just sold some old books."

"Books are worth this much?"

"Some are, yeah."

"I guess I should start reading huh?"

"Wouldn't hurt."

The journey back to New York City took significantly longer than the journey up the night before, as it was the middle of the day, so Harlon took his time and stopped on the way for some lunch. By the time he closed the front door to his apartment, he was tired and his ass ached from driving so long, so he went to his bathroom and soaked in the tub until the water got too cold for comfort. Over a light snack, he thought about the money Rink-Standen's books had brought him and how he should use it. After recouping his outlay on the mirror there was still plenty left and he pondered his options as he ate. A holiday perhaps, new car, redecorate the apartment, or invest it for the future? As he made his way to the closet, which he now called his Psychomanteum, he had decided to invest half, which would add nicely to his retirement package, and after having the apartment redecorated, flutter the rest on the stock market. If he made a fortune, all to the good, but if he lost the lot, he would not worry. It would be fun, and there was always the chance that he would make some more.

The shadows moved, slowly oozing down the front of the mirror before turning back on themselves and swirling back up to the top and around. It reminded Harlon of all the television footage he had seen of weather patterns seen from the space station, only this was dark not white. He was determined to remain in his seat no matter what happened, and he held his gaze soft as the shadows gained in solidity as they slowly roiled over the surface of the mirror. The room was no longer a boring shade of mustard yellow, but grey and he noticed as he gazed that the grey was not one uniform shade, but multi toned. Like a thunderous sky, it slowly oozed into the tiny room and swirled in the empty space between the mirror and Harlon's chair, the whorls and loops creating a visual distortion that gave Harlon the impression that he was falling. The shadows swirled as Harlon sat, one moment falling through the spinning grey tunnel, the next, flying through a thunderous grey sky.

As Harlon flew and fell and relaxed into this new experience, the shadows changed. He became aware that he was not alone within this grey roiling fog, but he saw nothing, and his resolve to continue without giving in to fear, held firm. Something touched his mind, but only for a fraction of a second, and Harlon was surprised, but elated. For a split second, another mind had linked with his own, of that he was sure, but he did not know how he knew. The only way he would be able to describe it later, was that for a micro second, he was not alone in his own head. The sensation was gone as quickly as it had appeared and Harlon continued to sit, willing the shadows to grow and strengthen. He was sure that if things continued to progress as quickly as this, and with his strength of mind to resist fear, he would reach Patricia Drake and finally establish communication.

A tendril of shadow gently reached towards him, but this time he remained steadfast, forcing his mind to relax. The tendril made contact and Harlon's mind opened wide under its weight. The darkness swept inside and examined every nerve fibre, synapse and molecule. It swept away his fears and replaced them with something else, something that should never have been there, but which once installed, set him on a road to damnation.

PSYCHOMANTEUM

5

It waited patiently for the Portal Keeper to return, knowing without a doubt that he would. It detected within his energy a determination to seek, to find out at any cost and It knew that this was his weakness. It would use this weakness to maintain an open portal so that travel between Its own domain and that of its opposite would be available whenever necessary. The Portal Keeper did indeed return, but when It tried to make contact in order to secure control, his fear was stronger than his resolve and he broke the already tenuous connection, forcing It back. It continued to wait, ever confident in the human's return.

When he did indeed return, It resolved to take care until control had been established. It did not want to lose this Portal Keeper, for the energy given off by his mind told It that he would be easy to control. It waited until the man's energy signalled that he was open and willing to be approached before reaching beyond the portal. With care, It embraced him in its outer energy field, and allowed him time to let down his guard further before reaching for his mind. Deftly It reached out a tendril of energy and sliced effortlessly into his mind. Once inside, It probed deeply into every cell, through every membrane and along every blood vessel. It felt his feelings, watched his thoughts and then finally, found the right spot to install a tiny portion of Its own core energy. No more than a particle, a thousand times smaller than an atom was all it took to take over control of the Portal Keeper, and once there, Harlon and It were one.

Once the man was asleep, It roamed the building, getting its bearings. Everything here had changed since the last time, and the humans, there were now so many of them. The fetid smell of life was everywhere, the all-encompassing lust to continue living was painful to It, and it was some time before the reason for this made itself clear. These creatures who represented Its opposite, Its nemesis, were now much more numerous than on Its last sojourn here. The sheer number of them now made the journey beyond the portal a dangerous one. That smell, the foul odour of the longing for life was not only unpleasant, it was deadly. It knew that it must keep its journeys here brief to avoid damage. With that in mind, and having gained all there was to know about the layout of the building, It flew through the various rooms and corridors in search of a suitable food source.

Saul Benedict licked his lips as he pinned the photo to the wall, his secret wall of pleasure. There were seven now, and he was becoming more expert each time. His groin hardened as he allowed the recent memories to flood back, and he had his zipper halfway down before he heard the sound. Instinctively zipping back up, he turned, flipping the curtain across to hide the pictures as he did so. He went into the hallway and his heart flipped in shock as he saw his front door standing open. After checking each way down the corridor, and seeing no one, he shut and locked the door before searching every room in his apartment. When he was sure he did not have an intruder, he returned to his wall and reached up to pull the curtain back.

The sound made him spin round, and he just had time to notice something glinting before the pain took hold and gripped him. The knife, the large one he had spent over fifty dollars on was embedded so far into his chest that it pinned him to the wall behind, his wall of pleasure. Terror took hold and squeezed his throat. Saul tried to scream, the blood that filled his mouth and trickled down his chin preventing him from making any sound. That sound came again, and another of his knives danced on the counter top, spinning round and round before flying through the air and embedding itself through his abdomen three inches above his navel. As the knife, held by no hand that Saul saw, sliced downwards towards his groin, he thought he saw a fat grey figure standing in the shadow in the corner, but darkness overwhelmed him before he determined if it was real or a shadow.

6

Harlon awoke, threw back the sheet and forced himself into a sitting position. Sweat soaked the sheets and plastered his hair to his head, which throbbed painfully. Swinging his legs to the floor, he took a long draw from the water bottle he kept on his nightstand before hauling himself to the bathroom. Gazing at his reflection, it took a moment for him to recognise himself. The normally bright eyes were now black ringed and hooded, his skin had lost its usual healthy tanned glow and was now pale and waxy. Assuming he had caught a cold from someone at work, he swallowed a couple of pills and took a shower.

It was as he was drying himself that he realised he could not remember leaving the Psychomanteum and making his way to bed the night before. Putting the towel back on the rail, he forced his mind back to his last memories of the previous evening. He remembered going into the Psychomanteum and settling down, he remembered the illusion of flying and falling caused by the roiling grey smoke and how exhilarating it was. Then he remembered being momentarily scared as something reached towards him, and how he had forced himself not to give in to the fear and react. After that, everything was gone. The important thing was that he successfully got himself back to bed without any problem, so why worry, he reasoned. No doubt as he became more experienced in the Psychomanteum, he would gain more control over his memory retention. After ringing his colleagues to say he was taking the day off sick, he dragged himself out to the store for supplies.

It was a warm morning and the sun revived Harlon as he walked the few blocks to the store. He decided on a whim to stop in at the coffee shop and treat himself to a full fat latte and slice of vanilla cake, and sat down without guilt. Having caught a bug off someone, he reckoned his body deserved some pampering, and enjoyed the treat immensely. The store was packed with shoppers, and Harlon finally emerged with his purchases after an hour. He hated shopping and made a point of breathing his germs over as many of the women in the checkout line as he could. Back out in the warm sunshine, he closed his eyes, letting his mood calm before strolling back towards home.

The police car was parked right outside the entrance to Gainsford House, which did not immediately catch Harlon's attention. What did make him stop in his tracks and gape open mouthed, was the slightly overweight police officer who leaned against the hood as he vomited into the gutter. Once he had brought up his breakfast, he fumbled in his pocket for a handkerchief and wiped his mouth, before reaching into the vehicle and grabbing the radio. Harlon could not hear the conversation in its entirety, but he did hear the officer talk about a DB. What does DB mean? He frowned and decided to ask the concierge. The welcome cool of the air-conditioned lobby embraced him as he entered and saw George, the maintenance man, looking decidedly grey. He was sitting at the desk and being offered hot coffee by an obviously concerned concierge. Curiosity got the better of him, and he wandered over.

"What on earth's the matter, George? You look awful."

The concierge frowned. "Oh hello, Mr Drake. Something terrible has happened. You won't believe it. There's been a murder."

"What? Here, in Gainsford House?"

"Yeah, and just a day or so after Mr Morrison's intruder. George here found him when he went to fix the waste disposal unit."

"Jeez," Harlon hissed, unable to articulate his incredulity more clearly.

"It was awful, Mr Drake," George said as he wiped his brow and took a sip of the coffee. "Pinned to the wall he was, with his guts all hanging out and blood everywhere. I'll be seeing it for the rest of my life, mark my words."

"Pinned to the wall?"

"Yeah," nodded the concierge. "By a knife. Stuck right through his chest and into the wall."

"Holy shit. Who was it?"

"Mr Benedict on the fifteenth floor. The guy with the ginger beard and bald head who never smiles."

"Oh yeah, I've seen him a couple of times. Was anyone else hurt that you know of? Has anyone else reported anything?"

"No. I've been round, called into every apartment, and warned everyone that there was a death, and that the police will be around and may wish to speak to them at some point, and no one reported anything suspicious to me. There are four apartments empty; two are on holiday, one is visiting a sick relative in Canada and another has just been sold. I got no reply at a few apartments, yours being one, Mr Drake, so I left notes asking those residents to telephone down to me at their earliest convenience. As far as I can tell, Mr Benedict was the only victim."

"I guess I'm going to be updating my security," Harlon remarked.

"Good idea," George replied. "And I won't be surprised if I find myself pretty busy for a while, installing locks and chains and goodness knows what else? At least it will help keep my mind off the sight of him, just dangling there on the wall like that."

"If you need anyone to talk to, you call in on me anytime, George, okay?" Harlon said and the old man nodded. "I mean it. We're a family here so don't be shy."

"Thank you, Mr Drake."

One hour later, Harlon put down the phone. It had cost him a substantial amount of money to persuade the home security company to agree to come out the next day and change the locks and update his security, but he was not going to argue. Now that someone had been killed, the cost was not an issue. Harlon had never felt insecure in his home before, and he did not enjoy this new insecurity. He made himself some lunch and thought about the situation. On the one hand, he was suddenly afraid and vulnerable for the first time, but on the other hand, common sense told him it was a one off terrible occurrence and he had no reason to worry. Mr Benedict was someone Harlon had only met a couple of times as they passed in the entrance lobby or shared the elevator, and he had to admit that he knew nothing about him or his life. He was known as an unfriendly man amongst the other residents, but that was only because he did not make extra effort to mix with his neighbours. Harlon had never experienced him being aggressive in any way, so he had to acknowledge that he might not have deserved the label.

"Let's hope it's one of those unfortunate random acts," he said aloud as he poured himself another coffee.

Detective Lamora looked up at Gainsford House. How the hell would his wife react when he told her his boss had given him a murder case two weeks before they were due to fly to the Dominican Republic for their first holiday in ten years? She would probably have him sleeping on the couch for a month, he decided.

"Shit. Perfect timing asshole. When I find you, I'm gonna rip you a new one for this." He entered into the cool lobby of Gainsford House and sauntered over to the desk to introduce himself to the concierge. The worryingly young blonde man tried to smile, but failed. Angelo did not mind, he guessed that this was probably the most exciting thing the kid was ever likely to experience, so he let it pass as he flashed his badge.

"Detective Lamora."

"Oh yes, Sir," the kid nodded. "Someone told me you'd be coming. They told me to send you right up. Fifteenth floor, apartment eighty-nine. Turn left out of the elevator and down the end of the corridor."

"Thanks." The elevator muzak was quiet and he found himself humming along as he watched the digital numbers flashing on the screen above the door. With a ping, the door opened and he stepped out to the sound of voices from his left. He noticed security cameras at regular intervals that covered every doorway and the elevator, and made a mental note to get someone onto checking out the recordings. He passed the forensic team on the way down the corridor, and noticed a couple of them looking ashen. When he met the Coroner on her way out, he showed his badge and nodded.

"Detective Lamora, what can you tell me?"

"Not much," the blonde woman replied. "The victim was a white male, twenty seven years old, bald head and ginger beard. Died from extreme blood loss due to him having been disembowelled."

"Disembowelled?"

"You heard me correctly, Detective," she nodded. "There are two weapons in evidence at this time, both knives. One pinned him to the wall through his chest, and the other was used to disembowel him."

"My god."

"Oh I don't think he had much to do with this one."

"What about the time of death?"

"I'd say anytime between eight o'clock and midnight last night."

"Okay thanks. Anything else to shock me?"

"Hell yeah," she nodded. "I thought you'd never ask."

"Shit. Okay give it to me."

"You know those seven murders, the vampire murders?"

"What about them?"

"There are photos of all seven girls, taken after death, on the wall in there. There are newspaper cuttings about the murders, maps of the locations, his own drawings, strange symbols, all sorts of crap. If he's not the vampire murderer, I'll buy you dinner at any restaurant you care to name."

"So we may have a vigilante on our hands huh?"

"It's possible."

"Jeez. Okay, thanks."

"No problem. I'll be doing the autopsy tonight and you'll have my report sometime tomorrow."

"Okay," he nodded. "You okay?"

"Yeah, I'm fine. It's been a while since I've seen anything like this. Sometimes I wonder why I didn't become a waitress or something."

Angelo nodded. He often asked himself a similar question when his job brought him into contact with the worst of the crazy stuff that New York has to offer. "I know. Go have a drink huh?"

"I'm on duty till midnight."

"I won't tell if you don't. You deserve it today."

"I might just do that. Catch you tomorrow."

The metallic tang of blood was strong as soon as Angelo stepped through the door. Several cops were searching the apartment, and the photographer was still working away, the flashes lighting up the apartment despite the bright sun that poured in through the large windows. He recognised one of the cops and nodded.

"Hi, what do we have?"

"Hi, Angelo, how ya doin? Ray not here?"

"I'm okay thanks. Just wondering how I'm going to tell my wife that I've got a murder case two weeks before our first holiday in ten years. Ray's in court. The politician kiddy porn thing."

"Well come with me. This is something I've never seen before. He's through there, in one of the bedrooms." He led the way down the hall and stepped aside to let Angelo enter first. The body still hung from the far wall, still pinned through the chest with what looked like a huge carving knife. The rent in his abdomen flared open from an inch or so under the ribcage to the pubic bone and everything that had once been inside, was now outside. Trailing loops of intestines snaked down to mid-thigh, still held there by fibrous sheets of mesentery. A large pool of blood the colour of blackberry jelly soaked the carpet and Angelo noticed within it some dried and crusted areas amongst the lumps of clotted gore. He grimaced as he took in the scene and guessed he bled out within seconds. Inside the room, the smell of blood was overpowering, and he was aware of another smell mixed with it.

"What is that shit smell?" he asked.

"It's shit, Sir. The coroner said the weapon that was used to disembowel the victim, slit the large intestine too, which contains waste matter on its way to the bowel."

"Nice," Angelo replied. "And I was planning on steak tonight."

"Me too. Kinda lost my appetite now though."

"So what do we have on the wall?" Angelo walked towards the wall and tried to avoid stepping in the congealed blood.

"Photographs of all seven of the vampire murders. All taken after death. There's loads of newspaper clippings about the murders, hand drawn maps of the bodies' locations, and all these strange symbols too."

"Okay, don't let the photographer miss anything, and strip the place. He might've kept souvenirs of his victims."

"We're doing that already, don't worry."

"Is anyone checking the security camera footage?"

"It's already on its way to the precinct."

"Good. And is anyone knocking on doors?"

"Yeah, we have a team doing that now. If anything gets flagged up, you'll get the call right away."

"Nice job, thanks."

Angelo left the apartment and took the elevator back down to the lobby where the concierge still looked stressed. He strolled over and gave him his best friendly cop smile.

"There's gonna be cops all over this place for quite a while I'm afraid. We'll try not to get in anyone's way but we have to do our job. I apologise now if we annoy anyone."

"Oh don't apologise, Officer. Anything at all you need, just ask. If we can help in any way to get this sorted, just shout."

"Thanks," he said. "Are you okay?"

"It's just that you never believe anything like this will happen do you?" the lad replied. "I mean, we all know it does happen, this is America after all, but you don't think you'll ever come into contact with something like this. It's most disturbing."

"Yes it is. By the way, how is the guy that found the victim?"

"Oh he's having an interview with a police officer now. They said they'll put him in touch with a counsellor too."

"Good. Okay, thanks for the help umm, sorry what's your name?"

"Jackson Marlow. You're welcome, Officer."

PSYCHOMANTEUM

Angelo left the lobby and went out into the early afternoon sun. Taking a deep breath of New York's exhaust filled air, he thought about the scene in apartment eighty-nine. This was already looking like it would be the strangest case he would ever work on. Despite the gory scene, there was something else that chilled him, and although he could not put his finger on what it was, he knew that genuine evil had visited this place. Over the years he had been in the force, Detective Angelo Lamora had seen things no one is supposed to see, but today, for the first time, an icy finger traced its way down his spine. With a shudder, he got into his car and drove back to the precinct.

PSYCHOMANTEUM

7

Angelo studied the photographs on the pin board in his office, his partner Ray Stellman beside him. The seven photographs that used to hang on Saul Benedict's wall, now gazed sadly at the two Detectives. Each of the seven women had been found raped, murdered, posed, and covered in symbols painted in their own blood. Twin wounds on their necks had earned their killer the nickname the Vampire murderer, and over the fourteen months since the first victim was discovered, the police had not found a single trace of who the murderer might be. Other photographs on the wall showed the symbols in detail, all of which had long ago been identified as occult symbols of various kinds, but no link between them had been found. Saul Benedict's hand drawn maps, together with the newspaper clippings and all the other various leads gathered over the fourteen months, filled the pin board. A photograph of Saul, as he had been found in his apartment, hung in the centre of the board.

"We can't assume he's the Vampire Murderer," Angelo said. "If the weapon we found in his apartment doesn't match the victim's wounds exactly, then we've nothing else to link him to the murders."

"Except the fact that he's collected all these newspaper clippings, drew maps of where the bodies were dumped, photographed them in situ, and then hung all that on the wall in his spare bedroom," Ray replied, gazing at Angelo wide eyed.

"A good lawyer could argue that he stumbled across the bodies by accident, and decided to take a few photographs. A little morbid perhaps, but we can't prove otherwise. People do that sort of thing all the time."

"Yeah I know, I know," Ray rubbed a hand through his hair. "This is our guy, we all know he's our guy."

"Of course we do, but we can't prove it in court without that screwdriver matching the wounds on the victim's necks."

"So we just wait for forensics."

"And pray, that wouldn't hurt."

"I got a couple of guys onto checking his background," Ray said as he poured himself a coffee. "He worked for a company that services computers for small businesses. His working day was usually spent visiting business premises, servicing their computers, installing new computer equipment etcetera, so there should be a solid paper trail of his movements. We're already sorting out a warrant for those records."

"Have they found out anything interesting so far?"

"Well he's an only child. His parents live in Kentucky. He spends Christmas with them every year, remembers all the family birthdays, yada yada yada."

"A model son."

"Exactly," Ray nodded. "Only this one murders young women in his spare time, jabs them in the neck with a screwdriver, paints occult symbols on their naked bodies with their own blood, poses them in provocative ways, and photographs them. Yeah, a model son."

"Does he have a record?"

"A couple of minor traffic violations, which isn't unusual in New York City, given how he earned his living. Nothing to excite us though."

"Is anyone going through his own computer?"

"Yeah. Ted's doing it now."

Angelo was about to reply when the phone rang and he jumped to answer it. Both were waiting impatiently for the coroner to call, and both prayed this was her.

"Detective Lamora?" a woman's voice asked.

"Yeah, speaking."

"This is Julia Mathers, the coroner. We met yesterday at Gainsford House."

"Yeah, hi," Angelo said and winked at Ray. "What do you have for me?"

"Can you come down here?"

"We're on our way."

Harlon was on edge all afternoon, and his mood was not made better by a throbbing headache and sweating. After dining lightly on cold chicken and salad, and a cool shower that helped him feel a little better, he sat down with a coffee to think. Being under the weather had made him decide not to sit in the Psychomanteum this evening, he probably would not be able to relax sufficiently anyway. Either that or he would fall asleep, so he decided to give it a miss until this cold, or whatever it was, had gone. The knowledge that a few floors above him someone had been murdered and left there, bleeding everywhere, creeped him out. He knew without any doubt that he would be sleeping with the light on for a while. A thought then occurred to him, that if indeed there was life after death, that Mr Benedict's spirit might come through the Psychomanteum and tell him who killed him. Harlon was intrigued at this possibility, but knew he would have a hard time explaining how he came by the information when the police questioned him. He would either be passed off as a crackpot, or arrested on suspicion of being the murderer, and as neither of those scenarios particularly excited him, he decided against reporting anything if such information did come his way.

This train of thought then led him to think about his own mortality. Harlon had never thought about his own end in any depth, apart from hoping it would turn out not to be painful. Now he did and although he would rather not die just yet, it would be interesting to finally find out the truth. It was not death itself he feared, but the method of dying that was cause for concern. The thought of ending his days in a similar manner to Mr Benedict in apartment eighty-nine, horrified him. Not because of the dying itself but the fact that someone else would be the cause of it. It was the aggression, the naked disregard for life that terrified Harlon. A fresh cup of coffee revived him and he decided that although he loved life, death intrigued him too, and that if he were to die, he would not fight it.

Sleep crept up on Harlon so slowly that he never knew what was happening. The leather couch was so comfortable, especially when he sat back and rested his legs on the matching footstool. There was a movie on the television that he had planned to watch, so he was determined not to fall asleep, but it could not hurt to get more comfortable, especially as he was sick. His last thought before his eyelids closed, was to hope there was to be no more trouble at Gainsford House. The dream was slow at first, the images patchy and disjointed. These patches were connected by episodes of blackness during which Harlon felt as if he were being controlled, manipulated in some way. Walking along his hallway, his legs heavy and his head swimming, reaching out to steady himself with a shaking hand, standing before the door to his Psychomanteum, and being aware of a dark pulsating energy from behind the closed door. His mind seemed split; one half knew he did not want to be doing this, while the other was excited by it. Despite his misgivings, he was thrilled beyond explanation, even physically turned on by it. Another period of nauseating and frightening blackness, then the door to his Psychomanteum stood open before him. Through the gloom he noticed the chair waiting to receive him and he sat, despite half of his mind knowing he should not.

37

The mirror was lost behind roiling blackness. A dense cloud that churned and swirled, sending the hairs on Harlon's arms standing rigid. The energy poured from it, and the half of his mind that was afraid, screamed in terror while the other half reached out and beckoned to it. The cloud roiled and churned, then lunged for him and Harlon was lost within another suffocating blackness. He registered half of his mind whooping in exultation. His mind swept along corridors, and as is the way of dreams, he did not question how he was traversing the building, nor why he was able to fly through walls, ceilings and floors. As he flew, that portion of his mind that had been so terrified, calmed. Exhilaration coursed through him as the fear dissolved away. Like scenes from a movie, rooms came and went as he flew through the building, snatches of incoherent conversations reaching his ears, insubstantial and disconnected. The darkened room flashed by and he was reminded of the Haunted House fairground ride he went on as a kid. The darkened tunnel, flashing lights that revealed horrific scenes, sudden screams; he could almost have been back there right now, riding the Haunted House and wishing his friends had not dared him to do it.

One room that flashed past was a bedroom, and Harlon noticed a couple making love in the bed. For a moment his curiosity was piqued and he slowed to watch, but was surprised as revulsion and terror swept through his consciousness. He leapt away in shock. The couple's groping hands, sweaty bodies, and moans of pleasure seemed to sap his energy. Rather than turn him on, it was if his own life force was being drained away. In another, he saw a couple he recognised and stopped to watch. Mr and Mrs Durant were fighting, one of their regular screaming drink fuelled rants that Harlon knew several of their neighbours often complained about. He could not hear the words, the screamed accusations, nor their rage driven excuses. The voices were lost to him, but he was aware of the energy and the longer he remained within the hate-filled room, the more he strengthened. It was as if he grew from within with each passing second, his being pulsated with strength as he soaked up the negative energy. He could almost describe the feeling as sexual, and as Mr Durant lashed out at his wife, catching her square on the jaw and sending her crashing onto the kitchen table, Harlon gasped as the sensation of pleasure rushed through his groin.

More blackness, after which he found himself flying along more corridors, through more ceilings, the rooms flashing past like movie stills. The occasional scent of human occupation either excited him, or filled him with revulsion. Through another ceiling and suddenly Harlon saw the night sky above and bright lights of the city below, the noise of life going on debilitating to him. Here and there, a dark spot of energy pulsed within the poisonous soup of life and as he concentrated, the thrill of lives taken reached him. Delicious waves of aggression being released and uncontrolled madness washed over him as he spread his awareness as far as he could. One dark spot reached his energy and he focussed on it. It was close so he let it guide him towards its source. The dark alleyway a block to the south of Gainsford House was filled with dumpsters, old shopping carts, an abandoned Buick, and piles of rubbish. The girl was no more than seventeen or eighteen, and sat behind an over filled dumpster that stank of rotting chicken, crying her eyes out. The syringe in her right hand shook slightly as she tried and failed to find a vein, the darkness and her emotional state not helping her concentration. He soaked up her energy and knew that she had lost all joy for living. As he allowed himself to dwell upon her detachment from the will to live, something within him grew, swelled with strength and became powerful. A flash of white caught his attention, and Harlon watched the sharpened length of broken chicken bone sink into her abdomen. It tore downwards, crudely ripping the flesh open and allowing the contents within to spill out onto her lap. The sight disgusted and thrilled him and as the blood soaked its way through her jeans, pleasure rippled through him. He leapt awake as his penis exploded in his hand, sending gouts of semen spraying up his chest and onto the smooth black leather of the couch on which he still lay. He licked a drop of wetness on his lips and tasted the salty tang on his tongue as he gasped for breath and tried to come to his senses. He saw the open zipper, his penis and balls exposed and slick with his own emission, and groaned in disbelief.

"Holy shit what's happening to me?" he whispered aloud to the empty and now darkened room.

He sat up and rubbed his eyes, trying to reconcile what had happened. He had the most vivid dream, which not only blew the top off the weirdness scale, but he had seen a young girl be murdered with a broken chicken bone in an alleyway. That in itself was weird enough, but add the fact that the sight had given him the most incredible climax ever, and now here he was sitting in his darkened living room with his dick and balls hanging out and covered in his own come, and you have a seriously fucked up situation. The last time Harlon had a wet dream was when he was a teenager fantasising about Jeany Lerue, and although he had a healthy sex drive and masturbated regularly, it had been a long time since he had come with such a force, and never as a result of such a sickening image.

He got up, put his dick and balls back in, switched on the light and padded out into the hallway, not bothering to zip himself up as he intended to go and shower. Halfway down the hall, he stopped dead, the breath leaving his lungs as adrenaline flooded through him. He went cold to the bone with fear as he stood at the open door to his Psychomanteum. The dull light within was still on, and the chair was swivelled around to face the open doorway as it always is when he leaves it after a session. He knew that the door had been closed, for when open, it blocks the hallway and prevents him from passing. How had it been opened, and by whom? Why was the light on, when he knew he always switched it off when he finished? Remembering that there had been a gruesome murder a few floors above just hours ago and an intruder a day or so before, Harlon suddenly felt bone chillingly vulnerable and scared.

After more than a minute of standing still in his hallway, too scared to move, he shook himself and went around the apartment, checking every room and closet, and found the place empty apart from himself. There was no evidence of anyone else having been inside, apart from the Psychomanteum looking as if it had recently been used. After double-checking that the front door and all windows were firmly shut and locked, he went for his shower. Sitting in his dressing gown, Harlon ate his dinner and let his mind again drift back to his dream. The imagery itself did not worry him, but his strong sexual reaction to it did. He had never been the sort of man who was turned on by violence, but that dream had given him the most amazing sexual experience of his entire life. He thought maybe he was having a midlife crisis or something, and the recent murder had probably played with his mind, the fear having worked its way into his dream and got mixed up with his normal sexual drive. He decided not to worry about it, and drank his coffee as he watched the late news.

8

It was much revived from the killing of the murderer. The man's dark purpose, and his total disregard for life, ensured his energy was pure in nature and gave It some much needed strength after so long waiting on the other side of the closed portal. Fresh negative energy rushed around Its being and strengthened the lust for more. The Portal Keeper was nearby, just beyond the portal. It waited impatiently for him to come. In the end, It could not wait. When he dropped into sleep, the tiny particle of Its energy within his brain came to life and exerted control. The Portal Keeper was the only potential weak link, and the only possible way for Its plan to go wrong. If he became too afraid to re-open the portal, It would be unable to gain access to this world where the fetid stink of life had been allowed to run unchecked for far too long. If It were to be able to rid the world of this parasitic lust for life, and return it to a far more hospitable place, It needed the Portal Keeper's indulgence.

This human had a neutral energy that told It that he could easily be influenced onto the right path. He had no particular lust for life, but no desire to end it either, and this neutrality told It that he would be easy to control. Once he had become addicted to the power of negative energy, he would be only too happy to do Its bidding. Once It had forced the sleeping Portal Keeper to open the portal, It took his sleeping soul along as passenger on the excursion. It wanted him to experience first-hand the sweetness that comes from taking life and the seductive warmth as the new negative energy flows into and mixes with Its own. Once the human experienced the immediate increase in strength and personal power that results, he would be only too willing to comply. It knew the human had enjoyed the experience, It knew this via the tiny particle of energy placed there on their first meeting. This tiny particle was now markedly bigger than before, having grown in size as a direct result of their shared experience.

Once the Portal Keeper was returned to continue enjoying the experience, It rested and waited. It would not wait for long, for It knew that the energies of the world were out of balance. The sickening joy and poisonous lust for life had been allowed to gain in strength for far too long. There was much work to be done, and once It had grown to full strength, more of the living could be influenced away from the flagrant need to preserve life, and balance would be restored.

9

Nessie Bellinger sat up in bed and hugged her knees, her tears splashing onto the sheet noiselessly. She had been awake for a couple of hours, her dreams having been invaded by the spirit Patty's incessant pleading for her attention. The images the spirit brought forth were as horrific as the ones she showed her the other day, only this time, Nessy recognised some of them. Saul Benedict lived on the same floor of Gainsford House, a little way down the corridor, and Nessy had shared the elevator with him on a number of occasions. Patty had warned her right at the beginning to avoid him, as he was a bad man, and Nessy had obeyed. She refused to make eye contact with him when they met, and kept her communication to the bare minimum. The image she witnessed now though, the hellish scene that Patty brought through to her mind was one of utter carnage. She saw the knife pinning him to the wall, the bloody entrails hanging down his thighs, dripping blood and other bodily excretions down his legs and onto the floor. She smelled the blood mixed with the bowel contents that pooled on the floor, and she felt the entity that brought about this massacre.

Again there was an inhuman quality to the energy, but it was not evil she sensed. There was no sense of wanting to cause mayhem for its own sake, no mind twisted by a desecrated childhood wanting revenge, no human madness directing the actions. It was as if the darkness was more of a natural occurrence than a man made one. Something that was a part of life and not an intrusion upon it. Nessy sensed its connection with the world and knew it belonged here but did not know why. This was not some conjured demon brought about by the esoteric rantings of a lunatic. This darkness was of the earth as much as the light was part of the earth, as much as love, laughter and inclement weather. She also knew that this meant destroying it would be impossible, and she cried for her impotence.

The spirit, Patty, showed Nessy new images and took her mind's eye to new horrors. Nessy saw the young girl in the dirty alleyway, and sensed she was nearby. She saw the darkness approach, felt the numb chill as it drew near. The girl's energy, grey and devoid of joy from a life of struggling to survive, blended with that of the darkness and strengthened it. She saw the bloody chicken bone lying on the ground as the light rain fell, and sensed the girl's horror in her last moments. The last image once again seemed not to belong, but Nessy knew that not only did it belong, it was central to everything. The large black framed mirror flashed through her mind and was gone before she got a fix on where it might be or how it fitted in with everything.

"Why are you showing me all this?" Nessy whispered into the darkness. "What am I to do about all this?" She waited, but no answer came, and she knew that this was because there was nothing she could do to prevent this event from running its course.

"If I'm not to stop it or help, why tell me about it? Please, Patty, tell me." Again, she waited for an answer, any answer, but all she got was a single image. In the image, she stood before a mighty angel, his wings wrapped around her defensively as he raised his sword against an unseen foe. Nessy knew this was purely a symbolic image, for she had never believed that angels, as humans tend to think of them, actually exist. Patty was telling her that she would be protected from harm, that she would not become a victim of whatever the terrible chilling darkness was and that she would survive. How many more of her neighbours were to die, and how this would end, she could not know, but she hoped it was not too many. Given that Patty had made it clear that this thing, whatever it was, could not ever be destroyed, Nessy feared for everyone. She lay down and closed her eyes, willing her mind to quieten as she waited for sleep, and prayed for good to prevail.

Detective Angelo Lamora was halfway home when he got the call, and cursed aloud as he turned the car around and headed for the location he had been given. His wife had given him a hell of a time the night before, when he had admitted that their holiday might be in jeopardy with this new murder case, and now he was to be late home again. He dialled the number and waited for her to answer.

"Hi, baby, I'm gonna be late again. There's been another murder and I have to attend." He closed his eyes and yanked the phone away from his ear, her reply physically painful.

"I know, but it's the job and there's nothing I can do. We talked about this last night. I'll be able to make it up to you when this case is over. I promise okay? Have I ever let you down on a promise?" He prayed as he listened. Relief washed over him, drawing his full lips into a smile. "I love you too, baby, and

I'll let you know when I'm on my way home. Should I stop and get some take out on the way?"

The alley was cordoned off with tape, the lights from police cars lighting up the street and the faces of the crowd that jostled for position. Angelo saw Ray's car and searched for his partner in the dark of the alley. The narrow thoroughfare stank of rotting food and urine, and he mentally shrank as he strode between the dumpsters and piles of trash. Julia Mathers, the Coroner, was already getting to her feet and handing over the scene to the forensic team as he approached

He nodded as she met his eyes. "Hi, what have we got this time?"

"White female, between seventeen and twenty five years old, approximately a hundred pounds in weight, blonde hair. Disembowelled, and bled out."

"Shit. Just like our vampire guy."

"Yeah. She's been dead around four or five hours at a guess. I'll do the autopsy first thing in the morning and you'll have the report by the end of the day."

"Okay, thanks."

"No problem. Kinda puts me off that t bone I had planned for tonight though."

"I know what you mean," Angelo grinned.

"I'll call you when I have the report for you."

"Okay, thanks." Angelo said and watched her go, her backside swaying provocatively as she walked.

"You're a married man, close your eyes."

Angelo feigned surprise as Ray grinned at him. "Hey, there's no harm in looking. Anyway, what do we have here?"

"Forensics are just starting so it'll be a while, but I can tell you she was a drug addict, heroine most likely. We found an unused syringe in her lap and her arms show evidence of habitual drug abuse."

"Do we even know who she is?"

"No. No ID on her so we'll have to do a fingerprint analysis and hope she's in the system somewhere. I can show you this though." Ray held up the evidence bag for Angelo to see.

"What's that, someone's take out?" He peered at the broken bone, tiny shreds of unidentifiable meat still clinging to one end.

"It's the murder weapon, an animal bone, chicken most likely according to one of the guys."

"You mean she was disembowelled with a chicken bone?" Angelo said, his eyes wide with disbelief as Ray nodded. "Fuck. What kind of sicko are we dealing with here?"

"You reckon it's connected to the vampire guy?"

The forensic team had been able to identify one of Saul Benedict's own screwdrivers as the murder weapon used in all of the women's deaths, and the search of his apartment had uncovered a haul of souvenirs taken from each one. A lock of hair tied with bright red silk thread and their blood soaked panties, which had also yielded Saul's own semen. It was more than enough to identify him as the Vampire Murderer, and a press conference was already being planned to take place once his family, and those of his victims, had been told.

"I don't know," Angelo replied, running a hand through his hair. "Disembowelment is not exactly a common method of murder, which might suggest there is a link, but until we know who this victim is and if she is connected with Benedict or not, we can't say."

"I know the official line. I've been a cop as long as you have y'know." He held Angelo's gaze to push his point home.

"I'd say it probably is connected, yeah. What do you think?"

"It has to be. How many disembowelled victims have you processed in your career?"

"One so far."

"Same here, the same one. So my guess is yeah, they're connected. Don't ask me how though, because I haven't the faintest idea."

"Once we get the girl's identity, we can begin to find out if she's linked with Benedict. Until then, we scratch our balls and hope there's no more. Is there a doughnut shop open around here?"

"Yeah, come on, it's my turn to buy," Ray said as they walked back up the alley.

Harlon awoke late, his head pounding. After a shower and a couple of painkillers, his head cleared a little, so he decided to go out for a walk to get some air. The sidewalk was crowded and he was acutely aware of bodies all around him as he negotiated his way down the busy street. The noisy chatter of a fat woman in a green dress behind him stabbed through his temples, and

Harlon wanted to yell at her to shut the fuck up. A young girl pushing a stroller passed by in the opposite direction, the kid screaming its head off and smelling strongly of shit and baby sick. It almost made him vomit, and he was relieved that she was not travelling in his direction. A man came out of a store up ahead and walked along ahead of Harlon with his cell phone to his ear. He was obviously not happy with the actions of some female known only to himself, for he repeatedly referred to someone called 'That Woman,' and expressed a strong desire to see her caused grievous bodily harm in all sorts of ways. In less than a minute, Harlon felt much better. His headache was almost gone and his stomach had settled. Maybe he should stop somewhere for a coffee?

Without warning, the man stuck his hand out and yelled something, and Harlon noticed a cab pull across the traffic and stop beside him. The man told whoever he was talking to, to wait a moment, while he opened the door and climbed in. After a quick word with the driver, the cab sped off and out of Harlon's sight. Almost immediately, the clamour of people's chatter hit him from all directions, ricocheted around inside his skull, and had his head throbbing painfully. Smells accosted his nostrils and made him gag. Cooking meat from the burger bar across the street, fumes from the traffic, sickly sweetness from the pastry shop he passed, and thousands of unwashed armpits and sweaty crotches. Above everything was a smell he could not identify, but which lay over everything else, and Harlon knew it came from the people themselves. He did not know what it was, but it was disgusting and he knew that if he did not get away soon, he was going to puke.

Sweat poured from his brow and dripped off the end of his nose as he lurched into the alley between a clothes store and a coffee shop. The relief was swift and dramatic. Harlon was aware of the pain in his head dissipating before he reached the end of the alley. Leaning against the brickwork, he breathed deeply. What the hell was wrong with him? It was as if all his senses were suddenly switched to ten times their normal sensitivity, overpowering him. The colours from store windows were so bright it was painful to look at anything other than the grey of the sidewalk. The endless chatter from thousands of voices, vehicle engines, music from the bar he passed, it all rammed into his eardrums until his head throbbed. The smells were the worst. He knew the city was a smelly place but he had no idea it was that bad. His next problem was how he was going to get back home again without making a spectacle of himself by puking on the sidewalk. He had only walked three blocks but it might as well have been three miles.

Having decided to jog home, to make the journey quicker, Harlon took a deep breath and left the alleyway. Trying to close off his mind helped a little, but the clamour of chatter from passers-by kept interrupting his focus, and by the time he had jogged one block, he was suffering. A few minutes later, he saw a middle-aged man walking along with a boy of around six or seven years old, and heard the man call him Timmy. As Harlon focussed on the boy, his physical discomfort melted away, and did not return until they entered a bookstore. He remembered the man talking into the cell phone had the same effect upon him. Why should that be? Before he formulated any kind of understanding, his stomach churned. He set off at a brisk jog and tried to bring the images of the cell phone man and little Timmy into his mind as he ran. Amazingly, it helped, and he reached the entrance to Gainsford House without having brought up his guts. Running into the cool of the lobby, he leaned against the wall, closed his eyes, and heaved deep breaths.

A voice cut through his concentration. "You all right, Mr Drake?"

Harlon opened his eyes to see George, the maintenance man frowning at him. "Oh hi, George. Yeah, I'm okay thanks. I think I've caught a bug or something."

"You don't look well at all. I'd rest up if I were you. When I was a boy, my mother would always put me to bed, open a window, and feed me chicken soup every three hours."

"Did it work for you?"

"Don't know, but I've never been able to stomach chicken soup ever since."

"I guess not then."

"You need some help up to your apartment?"

"No, I'll be okay now I'm back in the cool. I guess the sun got to me. Thanks for asking." Harlon straightened up and walked towards the elevator, George's well wishes ringing in his ears. Now he was away from people, it was as if nothing had been wrong.

10

After a light lunch and some much needed housework to clean the apartment, Harlon sat down to think about his morning's experience, and try as he might to be objective, he was worried. The more he thought about it, the more he realised that it was his close proximity to the people that had made him so ill, and that once he was away from them, he felt better immediately. There were the two people whose presence affected him in a different way though, the cell phone man and little Timmy, and Harlon concentrated his thoughts on them and what was different about them.

The cell phone man had been angry, judging by the part of the conversation Harlon heard, and he had been aware of the angry energy pouring from him. Harlon had not noticed at the time, as ill as he was, but now he was able to concentrate, he remembered the cell phone man had given off a tangible air of anger and desire for revenge. It had washed over Harlon, enveloped him in a blanket of negative feelings, and the effect had been wonderfully cathartic. The moment he got into a cab and drove away, taking his negative energy with him, Harlon had become ill again until he was able to escape down the alley.

Harlon frowned as he tried to make sense of everything. No one had ever expressed the opinion that Harlon was the type to thrive on negativity. He had always loved life and had many friends whose company he had always enjoyed. Negative people were something he had always made an effort to avoid as he found their energy disruptive and chaotic. Harlon was a peace lover, a meditator. So why was cell phone man, with his strong negative energy, the only thing that kept Harlon from being ill?

The kid, Timmy, was Harlon's next point of concentration, and at first, he was tempted to dismiss any notion of him being negative. Then he remembered catching a look that passed across the kid's face as he and the man who held his hand negotiated their way through the crowd. Someone bumped the kid's arm as they passed, and Timmy looked at them as they disappeared on their way, letting Harlon catch a glimpse of his face for a moment. The only way Harlon could describe that expression in hindsight, was to say it was like a darkness that swept from the kid's eyes and spread over his face. Seconds later it had gone as he turned away, urged on by the man tugging at his hand. As he followed behind them, Harlon remembered feeling that same darkness pouring off the kid and flowing over him as he walked in its wake, only this darkness was stronger than cell phone man's darkness. Little Timmy already had the negative energy of the evil man he was to grow up to be. Various scenarios raced through Harlon's mind. What was Timmy to become and how was his evil destined to be displayed? Serial killer? Child murderer perhaps? Harlon shuddered and shook the thoughts away. It was only because he was so ill at the time that he did not notice the easy natural way in which both Timmy's and cell phone man's dark energies revived him. He was so desperate for anything that might give him relief that he soaked up the cure without knowing what it was. Only now, in the quiet peace of his own apartment, could he look back objectively and see with clear-headed truth.

"What the fuck is happening to me? Am I going crazy?"

Harlon was sufficiently worried that he decided to go and take another walk to reassure himself that he was not going mad, so he got up and left the apartment before fear made him change his mind. Maddy was concierge today, he noticed, and she gave a polite smile as he passed the desk.

"Good afternoon, Mr Drake. Lovely day out there."

"Hello, Maddy. Yes it is." Through the thick glass door, he saw the tide of people flowing past in both directions, and memories of that morning's excursion flitted through his mind. Harlon took a deep breath and pushed them away before reaching for the door. After the air-conditioned interior of Gainsford House, the humidity hit him like a hammer as he hopped down the steps and into the flow of pedestrians. Before he made it half a block, Harlon recognised the first symptoms taking hold. His stomach fluttered sickeningly, made worse by the fact that his lunch was now inside it and churning. Sweat trickled down his brow and wetness under his armpits made his shirt stick to his skin. A tickle in his temple soon became a powerful throb and Harlon regretted having chosen to make this excursion. Remembering his train of thought from earlier, he tried to block his mind from the people around him, and pictured himself within a darkened room, inside a big darkened house, set in the middle of hundreds of acres of lonely countryside.

The people flowed around him, but within his mind, Harlon was alone in the comforting darkness, with no other person for miles. This imagery made a big difference while he concentrated on it, but in order to walk down the street without bumping into people, walking into a post, or being run over, he had to allow himself to be aware of his immediate surroundings. This meant that his awareness of reality was at odds with his mind's imaginings, making it a constant battle for dominance between the two. Harlon stumbled and people stared at the obviously sick man stumbling along the sidewalk. Embarrassment stung his cheeks and took centre stage within his mind, which made his ability to keep the healing mental images strong in his mind, more and more difficult. Another half a block and an alleyway appeared to his left, blessedly abandoned. With a sigh of relief, he lunged down it and slumped against the side of a dumpster. Within seconds, the miserable sickness flowed away and normality returned, so he opened his eyes to investigate his surroundings. As he looked around the alleyway, he saw the police tape hanging limp from the dumpster opposite, the remains of tape marks on the ground and he recognised where he was.

All at once, he was back in his dream from the evening before. The chill of the night air making the tiny hairs on his face stand up as he flew through the air. His ears rang with the sounds of engines, vehicle horns and angry voices, mixed with music from a nightclub and cheers from a nearby bar. Smells, discarded fast food, piss, vomit, all mingled one upon the other as he returned to the moment behind his closed eyes. Images flew through his mind as he gave himself up to the disturbing memory. She was there, the young girl barely out of her teenage years knelt down in the lee of the dumpster. The cheap clothes said thrift store, the over made up eyes and smudged glitter nail polish gave away her origins at the poor end of town and hinted at her dream of moving somewhere better. The syringe in her hand told him she had long since given up chasing her dream, and would probably deny ever having had such ambitions. Desperation poured from her and enveloped Harlon as he remembered from the night before. A few short years of bad parenting, even worse education, the wrong friends and no idea how to change any of it, brought her to this moment. A smelly alley and a syringe was the sum total of her life and she had no more strength left to fight. She wanted peace and cried for the wasted years as she prepared to embrace whatever waited for her. Without warning, a flash of white caught her attention and her eyes widened in shock. The broken chicken bone, its long edge razor sharp lunged towards her. With a grunt, Harlon's body convulsed, and his mind returned to the moment. As he sat behind the dumpster, his hand wet with his own ejaculation, he watched his penis discharge for the last time.

After cleaning himself up with his handkerchief, he zipped up and prepared to make the journey back home. With the aid of his mental imagery, which now included the girl being slashed with the chicken bone, Harlon made it back to Gainsford House without vomiting in public. The problem was he got a noticeable erection whenever he dwelt upon the imagery of the girl for too long, but a hard on in public was slightly better than puking in public. The cool of the lobby together with the relative quiet of the interior revived him immediately and he made for the elevator, convinced he was either having a severe mid-life crisis, or going crazy.

Harlon slept away the rest of the afternoon, a seemingly dreamless void that served neither to refresh nor revive, and awoke at sunset heavy and lethargic. A shower and change of clothes helped a little, but he was still unsettled. It was as though his whole life had been turned upside down. A few days ago, he was excited by his new hobby, his Psychomanteum that had offered the possibility of communicating with Patricia Drake, the ancestor that intrigued him so. He had allowed his focus to slip away, so Harlon decided to get back on course and refocus on what had been his new interest a few days ago. Hoping that this would help him get back to being the man he used to be, he got up and headed for the closet in the hall.

He spent a few minutes concentrating his mind on what he knew of Patricia Drake, before closing his eyes and breathing deeply for a few minutes to relax his body and mind. Once he settled, he opened his eyes, gazed softly at the mirror, and waited for something to happen. The light dimmed a little and he noticed the surface of the mirror become fluid. Grey mist ebbed and flowed over this fluid surface as the already dull light dimmed further until he could not tell whether the low bulb was still glowing or had gone out. The mist flowed, churned, and roiled over the fluid surface of the mirror before gently flowing from its edges and into the room. Shades of grey too numerous to count, from almost white to deepest black, swirled around the room and embraced Harlon into its depths, and he relaxed into it.

The body of Harlon sat in the chair within the Psychomanteum without moving for almost three hours. What was left of his own free thinking mind was trapped deep within, a prisoner of a dark force of immense power. As if half asleep, he watched the events unfold but was powerless to switch his attention from the images. He was aware of the dark force having taken full control of his mind, his decision making process was now beyond his mental reach and try as he might, he failed to will himself back to full control of his faculties. The dark force that controlled his mind linked so perfectly with his brain that its reactions and his own were indistinguishable, as if he and it were one being.

Just as on his previous times within the Psychomanteum, Harlon's mind flew through Gainsford House. This time it was as if he was physically there doing it and not sitting in the chair within the Psychomanteum dreaming it. The reality of it was unlike any of his previous experiences, and if he did not remember sitting down in the chair, he would swear he was actually flying around the building. He flew through walls, up through ceilings, and down through floors, the momentary frisson as he passed through the fabric of the building, strange but exciting. It was weird, the stone reacted to him in a physical way, even though he was not physically there, and he felt that reaction in his own physical body. Whatever manner of creature it was that now controlled his mind, Harlon knew that it was definitely not the spirit of Patricia Drake.

It had to be some dark entity, of that he was sure, for the darkness within it was thick, tangible. As he allowed his mind to dwell on the controlling force, he found that it did not just emanate darkness and negativity; it was made of darkness and negativity. There was no gender to it that Harlon could identify, but there was a definite knowledge of its own existence, a purpose that compelled it. Harlon was in no doubt that whatever this purpose might be, it was bad. Whatever it was, it needed badness to sustain its existence, and he knew that the more badness there was, the stronger it would become. Knowing that it had a definite purpose it followed, he probed as much as he was able with his own much weaker mind. The only thing he discovered was a conviction that all of human life was out of balance, out of control, and that it was necessary for things to be brought back under control again.

A finger of mist entered his mind and probed, gently at first until Harlon's resistance subsided, then it flowed quickly, sweeping away all that did not serve the proper purpose, and finally planted itself firmly at the heart, the core from where it could steer him, pilot him, subjugate him. Harlon was the Portal Keeper and as such, was the only one able to open the door to this dimension, but as a free thinking being of this dimension, the possibility that he could choose not to open the portal again was too big a threat. Although he was central to everything, he must be controlled, and as what was left of Harlon's own mind realised too late what was happening, the black mist closed around it.

Instead of actively engaging with people as on previous occasions, this time Harlon watched as the dark entity rose to the top of the building and settled there, without moving. It was some time before he saw it allowing tiny particles of its own dark energy to penetrate the fabric of the building, and once implanted, each one grew like an unseen evil fungus. Tendrils threaded their way through the stone, wrapping each cell within a cocoon of dark energy, reaching towards others like itself. Once they met, they embraced, and as one combined force, moved out in all directions, soaking every stone, floorboard, drywall, curtain and light bulb in an invisible pulsating darkness. Slowly, inexorably, this insidious darkness crept down through Gainsford House like dry rot, and as the residents went about their business, it cast its influence over them.

Cecilia Goodman turned onto her back and looked up at the stars as she floated. Her nipples hardened with the combined effects of the pool water and the evening air and she thought of her husband. Abraham Goodman owned a successful marketing firm, which meant he spent most of his time working and Cecilia resented it, despite enjoying the lifestyle his work provided. One such benefit was owning the penthouse apartment in Gainsford House, and the rooftop swimming pool that allowed her the sensual pleasure of swimming naked under the stars. Although well respected herself as editor of a well-known New York arts magazine, she wished her husband would hand over a little more responsibility to his colleagues and spend more time with her. She was sure he was having an affair, probably with some doe eyed stick insect at the office, and although it made her feel like a failure, she had long ago stopped shedding tears over it.

Instead of making an emotional scene, turning to drink, or going home to mother, Cecilia used her sharp brain and salted away as much money as she could from both her own income, and what she got from Abraham without his becoming suspicious. She worked hard and within five years, had an impressive nest egg languishing safely off shore for when the shit hit the fan, which she had planned for their twentieth wedding anniversary in eighteen months' time. The respect she earned from those in her field would ensure she would continue to be successful in work, and the discreet way she would bring her husband down, would ensure no stain would be visible on her. She would be the beautiful, dignified, wronged wife, and the whole world would take her to their hearts, while Abraham got what he deserved for being a cheating asshole.

"Your martini, Ma'am."

"Thank you, Gabe," she purred at the butler her husband employed. She enjoyed teasing him. "Bring it to me would you?"

"In the pool, Ma'am?"

"Yes please."

"Umm, this is my only uniform. The other one is still at the dry cleaners."

"Then take it off. Come on, I'm dying of thirst here."

She watched as the young handsome man put down the small silver tray and removed his clothes. She had never seen him without his uniform of black suit, white shirt and bow tie before, and was stunned by his physique. He obviously worked out, judging by his muscle definition, and she could not help but stare. He stood at the side of the pool in nothing but his expensive boxers, and when she finally tore her gaze away from his body and looked at his face, she found him smiling at her. She grinned back and watched as he dropped the boxers, stepped out of them and dived into the pool.

An hour later, their cries rang out into the night air as they reached their climax, the water making the whole event all the more sensual for them both. Cecilia was amazed at the easy way she had seduced Gabe, and had enjoyed every moment of it. Being a rich woman, she knew he would continue to be a willing conquest for her, so long as she treated him well and did not give him any reason to kiss and tell. If the sex was always this good it was worth the risk, she decided. They climbed out of the water, lay on the deck looking up at the stars and laughed at the situation they had both suddenly found themselves in, before Gabe rolled over and took her again. Later on, when they came out of the shower after their third lovemaking session, they both commented on how dark and cold the apartment seemed this evening.

PSYCHOMANTEUM

11

It waited beyond the portal, the microscopic atom of energy placed within the Portal Keeper's mind, ensuring continuous awareness of his movements. Although essential to Its plan, the Portal Keeper was potentially a weak link, so control had to be acquired quickly. He had responded perfectly when It took his mind along on the last excursion, the absorption of the girl's dark energy having the right effect upon him. It knew that he would find this new experience intoxicating and addictive, and would want to repeat it once his initial fear was out of the way. Tonight would see full control of his mind come firmly into Its keeping.

Now that It had a permanent position within the Portal Keeper's mind, all of his thoughts, fears, dreams and desires flowed into Its consciousness as if they were Its own. His obsession with the spirit of Patricia Drake intrigued It. Why would a mortal expend so much energy thinking of someone who was no longer in their world? Once embraced by death, they no longer exist in the physical world and to expend energy thinking of them seemed inexplicable to It. That strange and purely human affectation they call love had always been one of their strongest defences, and in order to defeat them, It always made an effort to study their nature. This one aspect was not only the strongest weapon in their arsenal, but also the one thing about them that It was never able to understand.

When the Portal Keeper was ready, It drew him to the portal and waited while he prepared himself. Once the portal was fully open, It sent tendrils of energy through to gently caress him without causing fear. It could, if desirous or necessary, force him into submission, but a willing keeper always opens the portal wider and quicker than one who has been forced through their unwillingness or fear. It knew that patience would bring the desired result, and as time was unknown to It, patience was Its nature. It waited until the Portal Keeper was relaxed and trusting before firmly cementing enough of Its own energy inside his mind to ensure his compliance. In taking over control of him, they became one being. The physical vessel through which It now had total control of the portal, and the pure energy, the unseen powerhouse behind. There would come a time when the Portal Keeper would not be needed. When the people were under sufficient control to produce a constant supply of negative energy to fuel Its permanent presence in the physical world, the man could be discarded. When that time came, the fetid stench of joy and love of life would be unable to cause damage, and It could continue to work unfettered. Satisfied, It flew through the portal to begin.

12

Roy Durant switched the television to his favourite show, lifted one butt cheek and farted loudly, before draining the last of the beer from the bottle in his hand. His wife, Donna, was in the kitchen washing dishes and singing, the noise putting him on edge. He turned up the volume on the television and sniffed, happy that her infernal caterwauling was now hidden from his notice. During the ad break, he shifted in his seat. He was cold despite it being high summer. Rising from his chair with a moan, he checked the air conditioning and frowned when he found it switched off. Turning around, he walked through to the bedroom and put a sweater on, before heading back to the television. Halfway down the hall, the lights flickered off, then on again, much dimmer this time than they had been before.

"What the fuck?" He flicked the light switch up and down a few times. No matter how many times he switched the lights on and off, they were dimmer than usual. He shrugged, the ad break was no doubt over by now and he was missing his show. He walked back through to the living room and sat down. The television screen was snow and Roy swore loudly, before walking over and thumping it several times, to no avail.

Donna came in and frowned. "Roy, the water's gone cold. I think the water heater is broken."

"Never mind that, the TV is fucked."

"The lights flickered too, just a minute ago," Donna continued, unperturbed by his dismissal of her.

"It's damn cold in here too. What did you do to break everything?" He glared at her.

She bristled. "Me? I didn't do anything. You were here too; maybe you broke it by fiddling with it." Roy said nothing, but his face darkened as he strolled over to where his wife stood in the doorway between the living room and kitchen, and punched her full in the face, breaking her jaw. Donna fell, but did not cry out. She got up silently, then walked back into the kitchen, took the largest of her frying pans down from the rack, poured in some oil and put it onto the stove to heat. Roy sniffed and went back to investigate the television, getting on all fours to see if any of the leads had come out at the back. After taking them all out and putting each one firmly back in, he switched on and scratched his chin at the snow that still covered the screen. Soft footsteps approached from behind, the slip slip slip of Donna's slippers on the carpet and he turned. She walked up to him as he knelt down in front of the television, waited until he turned around to face her, and poured the hot oil down over his head.

In the adjoining apartment, Roy Durant's screams went unheeded as Dale Millbank stared out of his living room window. In his hands, he held the body of Trixie, his Abyssinian cat who minutes ago had been purring softly in his lap as he listened to his favourite Mozart concerto. Dale closed his eyes and let the music sweep him away, and did not notice the lights dim and the temperature drop. It was not until he noticed that the music annoyed him that he opened his eyes and scowled at the animal on his lap. The music that always elated him was now forgotten as he took hold of Trixie and snapped her neck around in one clean movement, the crack of bones clearly audible but not registering within his mind. As if in a trance he stood, the body of Trixie in his hands and approached the centre window. For once, the view of night time New York did not excite him. Opening the window as far as he could, he cocked his head to the side a little, as if listening to something, and then with a nod, he flung the body out into the night air.

Slowly but surely, the darkness crept through Gainsford House, inch by inch, seeping into the fabric of the building itself. It soaked into the concrete and glass molecule by molecule, becoming a permanent feature of the building, inherent within every wall, ceiling, floor and window. Memories of laughter floated away, taking their joyful influence with them. Loving bonds broke, to be replaced with indifference, anger and hatred, and the residents soaked up this new influence. Immediately they changed, became willing producers of new and darker emotions, which in turn soaked into the fabric of the building. A deadly cycle of darkness came into being, a cycle that would take many of them on a journey to a place they could only imagine in their worst nightmares.

At ten thirty the next morning, Angelo laughed loudly at Ray's joke, and was about to reply with a quip of his own, when the phone on his desk rang.

"Homicide, Detective Lamora." He listened, his brow creasing into a frown before nodding. "We're on our way." Slamming down the phone, he grabbed his jacket and cocked his head to Ray. "There's an incident over at Gainsford House."

"An incident?"

"Yeah. Apparently, the guy on the desk called an ambulance when he noticed one of the residents had some kind of head injury. The medics arrived but are unable to gain access to the apartment. It seems the woman's husband is refusing to let them in to look at her. They've asked us to help them gain access."

"Okay. Let's go."

Both were hot and sweaty by the time they pulled up outside Gainsford House, the air conditioning in Ray's car having not yet been repaired, and both were reluctant to open the windows and breathe in more of New York's traffic fumes than they had to.

"You have to get that air con seen to," Angelo said as he mopped his brow with a handkerchief. I must've lost five pounds in sweat in that journey alone."

"It's booked in for Friday," Ray replied as they climbed the steps to the door and entered the cool of the lobby. Both welcomed the refreshing change in temperature and approached the desk.

Angelo noticed the worried look on the young concierge's face. "Detectives Lamora and Stellman."

"Oh yes. Apartment sixty-three, eleventh floor. The medical guys are up there, still trying to get in."

"Okay, thanks. Was it you who made the call?" The concierge nodded. "In case we need to get a statement from you."

"No problem. I'm on duty until seven." Angelo nodded and indicated to Ray, and together they headed for the elevator.

They heard the shouting the moment they left the elevator, and headed towards the sound. Three ambulance personnel were outside the door to apartment sixty-three, banging on the door and pleading to be let in to check out their patient. They showed their badges and the medics stepped back.

"Thank god you're here," a young black man said. "The guy is refusing to let us in to check on his wife."

"Are you sure your help is required here?" Ray asked.

"We're pretty sure, yes," a blonde woman nodded. "From what we were told by the maintenance man, we believe she probably has a broken jaw."

"And there's the guy's skin injury too," the young black man said.

Angelo frowned. "Skin injury? We were told that the woman was injured. No one said anything about a guy being injured."

"Apparently, the maintenance man was called up here earlier to fix the lights. He noticed that the woman, Mrs Donna Durant, had what looked like a serious injury to her jaw. He said she was covered in blood and swears he saw a bone sticking through her skin. He also noticed that the man, Mr Roy Durant, seemed to have suffered an injury to the skin on his face and head, which he described as melted and yucky looking."

"We need to get in there real soon," the third medic, a middle-aged woman with huge breasts, said.

"Okay let's see if we can do this nicely," Angelo said as he stepped forward and banged on the door. "Mr Durant. This is the police. Open the door so the medical people can make sure you're both okay."

The reply was swift and to the point. "Fuck off." Angelo raised his eyebrows.

Ray grinned. "You're too nice sometimes, let me. Mr Durant. If you don't open the door, we're gonna bust it open and take you down to the station. Then we'll give you a bed for the night with all the crazies and nutjobs. When we let you out in the morning, not only will you have a criminal record which will severely affect your credit rating and job prospects, but you'll have to pay for the repairs to the door."

"I told you to fuck off, asshole. Are you deaf or just stupid?"

"Now that's disrespectful don't you agree?" Ray said to Angelo, who grinned and nodded. "After three?" The two of them stood in front of the door, guns in their hands. Ray counted down and they had the door off its hinges on the second kick. The sight that met their gaze almost made Ray cry out in shock. A man of around thirty five or so came at them, his hands held out in front like claws, a guttural sound emanating from somewhere within the horribly disfigured face. Angelo just had time to think how accurate the maintenance man's description had been, when a woman's angry howl made him spin around.

Ray had Roy Durant in cuffs within twenty seconds, and held him down while the medics administered a sedative and strapped him to a gurney. Once he was contained, Ray looked for Angelo and saw him still struggling with Donna Durant, who seemed to have a superhuman strength. The two of them managed to cuff her and hold her while she was sedated, then called for a second ambulance.

"Just in case one or both of them wakes up before you reach the hospital," Angelo said when the young black medic protested that they had room for both.

Once both ambulances were on their way, Angelo asked the concierge to get the maintenance man to fix the door to apartment sixty-three. "And make sure you charge it to the Durants."

"I'll go and find him now," Ray said. "I'll get his statement at the same time. Meet you back here."

"Okay," Angelo nodded as he turned back to the concierge and prepared to take his statement.

Back in the comfortable cool of their office, Angelo and Ray compared notes.

"Okay so what did old George have for you?" Angelo asked.

"Well. He said he had multiple calls from the top four floors, all about lights not working properly, bad TV reception, faulty plumbing etcetera, and the Durant's were his eighth call. He knocked on the door and was surprised when Mrs Durant called out asking who it was. Apparently, she never did that before and George said it was odd, as several of the residents had appeared similarly reluctant to engage with him. When he announced himself, Mrs Durant opened the door and let him in. It was then that he saw her injury and asked her what had happened. She seemed oblivious to the fact that half her jaw was sticking through her face, and asked him to see why the lights wouldn't work properly. He then saw Mr Durant in the living room with his face all melted and when he suggested they call for medical help, they brushed off his concerns and said they were both fine. How did you do with the wide eyed concierge who hasn't yet come to terms with his sexuality?"

Angelo laughed aloud. "You're crazy."

"I bet you a hundred."

"You're on. Okay, well he said he had loads of calls from residents asking George to fix lights, check plumbing, fix air conditioners, and check out bad TV reception. Same story as George. George came down after visiting the Durant's apartment, and told him what he'd seen and suggested he call for an ambulance, even though the couple had said they didn't want one. He did that and when they arrived, he directed them to apartment sixty-three. A few minutes later, he gets a call from Mr Durant, threatening to knock his head off for calling them and saying he had no intention of letting them in. When the medics returned to the lobby, they asked him to call us."

"There certainly seems to be a right bunch living in that place," Ray said. "George told me that one old gal he visited to check the lights was muttering about evil spirits wandering the corridors at night, and how a black curse from hell has descended upon the building."

"A black curse from hell?" Angelo grinned.

Ray nodded. "Apparently, yeah."

"Sounds like my mother in law's cooking."

Ray was about to reply when the door flew open and Detective Peck rushed in. "Guys, you have to come and see this."

13

As the residents breathed in this new and invisible controlling force, they changed. Cecilia Goodman no longer silently brooded over her husband's indifference to her and plotted her own escape. Her pain and suffering, having been borne with quiet dignity, now boiled over as she willingly flung herself at their butler. A more than willing participant, Gabe laughed inwardly at the thought of selling his story to the media. Abraham Goodman had always been a good employer, had paid him well and he had always been fiercely loyal, ignoring his attraction to Cecilia. Now, as he thrust his way to orgasm for the third time, he could not imagine why he had been so loyal to this couple. He could not only enjoy fucking a gorgeous woman like Cecilia, but also make a fortune by either bribing her for his silence, or selling his story to the tabloids. If she wanted to repay him for his attentions by giving him gifts in return for his sexual favours, then he would keep quiet until he tired of her, but then, all bets were off as far as he was concerned.

One by one, the residents fell under the spell of this unseen force, and many found it a liberating experience. Those who normally dwelt close to the boundary between good behaviour and bad succumbed first, whilst those with more control over their base desires resisted for longer. Roy and Donna Durant, whose relationship had always been volatile, had no resistance at all and soaked up the negative influence like flies on a dish of honey. They exploded into violence unlike anything either of them had ever experienced before. Next door, Dale Millbank also succumbed quickly. Having suppressed a violent hatred of his mother since his own childhood, and the beatings he endured at her drunken hands, it did not take long for everything to come pouring out. Relationships had always been out of the question for Dale, his mother's treatment had made sure of that, but he had found an outlet for emotional bonding by keeping cats, who enjoyed his attentions and returned a semblance of affection he felt safe accepting. He had paid several hundred dollars for the pure blooded Abyssinian kitten he had named Trixie, and although a little aloof in nature, they had a good bond and she spent most evenings asleep on his lap. Dale suddenly realised that she was more of a nuisance than a joy. She was a supremely fussy eater, and the way she would turn her nose up and walk away from her dish annoyed the hell out of him. Whenever she used the litter tray in the bathroom, her shit stank up the whole apartment for hours, and her night time wailing kept him awake. He looked at Trixie and saw his mother, and all of his unspoken childhood torment came flooding out.

Halfway between the fourth and fifth floors, Rosy Newland skipped down the stairs and knocked on Doug Morrison's door, the hot dish in her hands becoming uncomfortable. She was about to knock again, when the door was suddenly yanked open, and Doug stood there with a face like thunder.

"What the fuck do you want this time?"

Rosy's mouth flapped as she tried to think of a reply. "Well I err, are you okay, Doug? I made you a casserole for your dinner tomorrow." She proffered the dish.

"Keep it, and don't bother making any more. Hasn't anyone ever told you that you're an awful cook? I'd get more nourishment casseroling my old army boots. Take it away and don't bring me any of your shit any more. In fact, don't come back at all, ever." The door slammed firmly in her face and Rosy stood, looking left and right, not knowing what to do. As the first tears of humiliation trickled down her cheeks, Rosy crept back upstairs to her own apartment, pleased that at least none of the neighbours had seen the exchange.

Inch by inch, the fabric of Gainsford House changed from a benign edifice of concrete and glass, behind the walls of which a diverse cross section of New York's humanity lived, into something darker. The negative energy brought with it minute cracks, which appeared first at the junctions of ceilings and walls like lesions on the once pristine faces of leprosy victims. The white painted corridors and stairwells slowly turned grey, the paint blistering and peeling under the weight of the dark energy. Dark spots appeared on the walls and ceilings, tiny at first like the freckles across the nose of an adolescent girl. From within these cracks and blisters a new change manifested. As the molecules of stone, concrete, glass, and wood, continued to succumb to the onslaught from the deadly parasite that now infested it, tiny beads of foul black snot formed. As the hours wore on, these individual tiny beads grew and one by one, they drifted from within the cracked plaster and blistered paint. As the foul smelling drops found others like themselves, they joined and traced their way down walls, windows, and doors. As the residents were succumbing to the control of this new negative force, so Gainsford House itself began to rot under its influence.

Within the apartments, tempers shortened and compassion faded as the residents gave themselves up to the influence of the new controlling force. None of them knew what was happening of course, it was all so natural to them. Arguments flared into all out rows, couples yelled and children screamed. The first signs that order was crumbling into chaos became apparent, but the people were oblivious to the danger. They dwelt in blissful ignorance of what was taking place, certain that nothing was wrong. If anyone had challenged them, all would claim they were the same as they had always been; such was the depth of their subjugation.

The seeds of darkness had been firmly sown within the fabric of Gainsford House, and the human residents' own natural emotional inclinations made sure that they fell under its spell. The walls built during years of social conditioning, behind which the baser aspects of human nature are kept, cracked under the influence of the negative energy. From those cracks poured years of pent up aggression, unsatisfied vengeance, and childhood trauma. Once breached, those walls would never be rebuilt whilst under this dark controlling menace. In giving in to their own negative drives, they fed it still further; creating a cycle of negativity that fed and grew like some crazy perpetual motion machine in a science fiction movie.

Angelo and Ray exchanged an astonished glance. "Have you ever seen anything like this before, Ray?"

"Hell no. I've heard of it though, a couple of times."

"We have to talk to this guy."

"I guess so."

"You guess so?" Angelo snapped, his eyebrows raised.

"He hasn't actually committed a major crime here. It's sick, but it's hardly even news worthy these days. We can't bring him in for anything except maybe public indecency, but with the murders that are going on, that's going to be a way down our priority list."

"Yeah, I'm aware of the law thank you. You have to admit though, with everything that's going on around this guy, this is weird. It's worth a deeper look at least."

"Absolutely," Ray nodded.

"Okay. Let's go talk to him. We have to interview Mr and Mrs Durant in hospital anyway."

"Right," Ray said as he stood and made for his office. Halfway there, Detective Suzy Shields called over.

"Hey Angelo, Ray, wanna know something really weird?"

"Sure, we love weird," Angelo grinned.

"A dead cat was found last night in the street below Gainsford House."

Ray frowned. "What the fuck has that got to do with us?"

"It belonged to a Mr Dale Millbank, of apartment sixty four, eleventh floor of Gainsford House. The veterinarian says that its neck was broken so much that its head was almost twisted off, and then it fell from the apartment window. There were pieces of what looked like human fingernails embedded in the fur of its neck. They reported it to us once they knew they probably had a crime victim on their hands."

The two detective frowned as they both tried to piece together the rapidly growing number of weird facts relating to Gainsford House and its residents. Angelo took the report from Suzy and thanked her, before reading it and showing it to Ray.

"So, we have a husband who broke his wife's jaw," Ray said. "And a wife who poured boiling oil over her husband's face. A serial killer disembowelled with his own kitchen knives, a drug addict disembowelled with a chicken bone, a guy jacking off at one of the scenes, and now some guy twists his cat's head off and throws it out the window? What the fuck is happening in that place?"

"A black curse from hell maybe?" Angelo offered.

"For once I don't think you're crazy."

The veterinarian showed them into his office and offered them coffee.

"You're here about the Abyssinian I suppose?" he asked. Angelo and Ray frowned. "The cat that was found below Gainsford House?"

"Oh, yeah," Ray nodded.

"Okay, let me show you the X rays first, and then you can see the body itself. Luckily she landed in a dumpster, which broke her fall and prevented too much further damage occurring which would've obscured the evidence of the crime. See here?" he indicated on the X ray, which clearly showed the skull and neck vertebrae. Pointing to a spot beneath the skull, he tapped the x ray. "The cervical vertebrae, the bones of the neck, connect to each other in two ways. Inter vertebral disks are soft fibrous cushions between each vertebra. See them here?" He looked at the two detectives, who nodded. "The articular joints are

68

tiny curved bones that fit into a socket in the neighbouring vertebra. See these shadows here? Those are the broken articular joints. Together with distinctive muscle and skin damage, it is obvious that this cat's head was twisted around so far it not only broke the bones in its neck, but it also snapped the spinal cord. To put it in simple terms, he twisted the head one way and the body another. In fact he almost severed the head, judging by the muscle and tissue damage."

Angelo let out a long slow breath. "Shit. Why would someone do that to a cat?"

"And are they doing it to people?" Ray added.

The veterinarian shrugged. "I cannot say, but here is my official report. I will be more than happy to testify against her owner in court by the way."

"Is this kind of thing common?" Angelo asked. "Do you see this type of injury much?"

"Unfortunately I have seen it before, a few times. I wouldn't call it common though, but certainly not uncommon. Why?"

"I just wondered how you'd rate this on a weirdness scale of one to ten."

"Well this is New York, Detective, so it wouldn't rate too high on such a scale unfortunately. A five, six maybe. Animal cruelty happens more than you think and more than I'm happy with. For some aggressors, it's the only way for them to exercise control in a life that often seems out of control to those living it. Some people who do this kind of thing to the family pet are wonderful parents to their kids. For such people, this outlet for their aggression keeps them from abusing their spouses or kids. For others, the darker kind, it's a stepping-stone on the road to becoming a serial killer. In between those two extremes are the out of control kids patrolling in gangs and trying to be tough, and all manner of crazies and psychos."

"Which one of those do we have here?" Ray asked.

The veterinarian shrugged. "You're the detectives."

Thirty minutes later, after seeing the body and collecting the fingernail pieces for forensics, Angelo and Ray set off to visit the Durants in hospital.

"Why would someone do that to a defenceless animal?" Ray said as he rubbed a hand through his hair. "I'm not really a pet kind of guy but this is wrong on so many levels."

Angelo nodded. "I hear ya. There's definitely some crazy shit going on up there in that building."

"My ex-wife was always on about moving out of the city, somewhere up state maybe, but I always refused," Ray said. "I was born and bred in New York and couldn't imagine living anywhere else, but things like this make me wonder if maybe I should've listened to her."

"Theresa's the same. She hates my job, although she's pretty good about it most of the time."

"How did she take the news of this case possibly ruining your planned holiday?"

"She yelled, I grovelled, and promised to make it up to her. Then she cried and I grovelled some more. Then we went to bed and had the best sex in months."

"So she took it pretty well then?" Angelo nodded and they both burst out laughing.

The traffic was slow, and they were glad to arrive at the hospital at last. Knowing that the building would be air conditioned, both were relieved that they could recover from being almost boiled alive in Ray's car in the journey over. After Angelo again complained about the broken air conditioner and another promise from Ray that it was booked in for repair on Friday, they headed to the reception desk and announced themselves. Finding that the Durants were in different wards was no surprise, so after admitting that Ray had a better way with the ladies, Angelo headed for the elevator to visit Roy Durant. The angry scene that met them when they assisted the medics the day before was still fresh in his mind as he entered the ward, and he prepared himself for a less than friendly exchange. What he got however, was the opposite of what he was expecting.

14

Roy's face was covered in bandages, an IV tube was attached to his arm, and the all-pervading smell of hospitals that always made Angelo uneasy, attacked his nostrils. He closed his eyes and tried to calm his rising anxiety, then introduced himself to the figure on the bed.

"Roy Durant?" The bandaged head turned towards him. "I'm Detective Angelo Lamora; we met this morning at Gainsford House." The head nodded slowly and Angelo noticed the eyelids blink. "Can you speak?"

"Yes."

"I need to ask you a few questions, but if you need a nurse or anything just say so and I can come back tomorrow."

"Could you give me a drink? There's some water on the side."

"Oh sure thing," Angelo replied and looked over at the nightstand. He noticed a glass of water with a straw and picked it up, carefully holding it so Roy could drink.

"Thanks," Roy said when he finished.

Angelo replaced the glass on the nightstand. "Mr Durant, both you and your wife committed a crime, and my job is to find out if either of you wish to file a formal complaint, and if so, start that process with you. Maybe you could start by telling me what happened and why?"

Roy avoided Angelo's eyes for long seconds before speaking, and the Detective guessed that something was deeply troubling him, something beyond a fight with his wife. He nodded encouragingly.

"It was like something took me over. Donna and I yell at each other sometimes sure, but I've never hit her before. I'm not a physical guy in that way, never have been. Last night though, something changed."

"What changed?"

"I don't even know how to describe it. I know how it felt, but I can't really put it into words. The only thing that comes close is to say that it was like something else was controlling my mind, and that something was evil."

"Evil?" Angelo asked. Inside himself, he groaned, assuming this was going to be another of those temporary insanity cases that never got anywhere near a satisfactory conclusion.

"Laugh all you want Detective, but I'm telling you that something bad is in that place, and I for one don't intend ever to go back there."

"Can you explain it for me? I can't just put something bad on my report or the guys at the precinct will have my balls."

"It was like a heavy darkness inside my head. At first, I thought it was just a bit of depression, but within hours it kind of, took over my mind. It gave me thoughts I've never had before, and although one part of me knew it wasn't me, the other part was stronger. I can remember being aware of this, thing, this darkness right up until the early hours, but by the time the sun rose, my memory had blacked out. It was like it took me over during the night, and I was aware of myself slipping further and further back as the hours wore on. I know George came to fix the lights, and I know medics were called, but I don't remember it like I was there. I can see the images of what happened, but there's no connection with them like in a real memory. I'm sorry I was rude to you."

"So you're telling me that you believe something controlled your mind, some kind of, unseen evil force?"

Roy nodded. "Yeah. No, I'm not insane, but that's how it was. Now I'm away from that place, I feel fine, like my normal self again. I won't go back there for anything, and don't be surprised if other people start acting weird too"

"Why do you say that?"

"Because before it took me over completely, it was like I could sense part of its mind as it melded with mine, and I know that me and Donna weren't its only priority. Whatever it is, it has plans for everyone in that place, believe me, Detective."

"Do you wish to file a complaint against your wife for domestic abuse?"

"No. I deserved this for what I did to her. I'm going to be scarred for life, and those scars will be a reminder to me what evil feels like, so I can resist it better next time."

"Okay. My partner is interviewing her right now, and until he's finished, I can't tell you whether she will want to file charges or not. Here's my card, call me if you change your mind or want to tell me anything more."

"Okay, thank you."

"Do you have somewhere to stay? A relative or something?"

"The doctor said I'll be in here for a while, but my brother lives in New York and I can stay with him until the apartment is sold."

"Okay. Can you give me his address so I can contact you there if I don't see you before they let you out of here?"

Roy nodded and Angelo jotted down the address, before saying goodbye and heading back down to the coffee bar to wait for Ray.

Angelo's coffee was almost finished when Ray appeared at the table and sat down.

"Hey," he said as he ran a hand through his hair.

"Before you say anything," Angelo grinned, "I'll bet you a coffee that my interview with Roy was the weirdest interview of either of our careers."

"Oh yeah?" Ray countered. "Well I'll match your coffee and raise you a doughnut every day for a month."

"So you got the evil possession thing too huh?"

"Yeah, you got it from Roy?"

"Yep," he nodded and read his notes aloud. Ray nodded all the way through before reaching for his own notebook.

"Donna said the same thing. A feeling of darkness became apparent during the evening, and as the night wore on, angry and violent thoughts kept coming into her mind. She said it was like there was another person inside her head, an evil person who wanted to do violent things, and she was powerless to make it go away as it was far stronger than she was. By sun up, she says it had taken her over completely and remembers seeing everything that happened as though it was on a TV screen, but she couldn't interact with what was going on, or stop herself from saying or doing anything."

"Same exact thing as Roy," Angelo said. "Does she want to file charges against him?"

"No. She's beside herself with shame at what she did to him, and she says she never wants to go back to the apartment. She says there's something bad at that building, something not of this world was what she called it, and she says she won't be going back."

"Roy too. He says he wants to sell up and move away."

"So at least we avoid having to deal with a domestic while this shit is going on," Roy said. You want another coffee?" Angelo nodded.

When Ray returned to the table, Angelo scratched his head. "All this talk about evil goings on is getting to me. Someone else mentioned it the other day, what was her name?"

Ray flipped through his notebook to find the entry of the conversation. "Mrs Hanny. You surely don't believe all this shit?"

"Whether I believe it or not is beside the point. They believe it, and that's why we can't dismiss it."

"Yeah, I get your point. So how do we proceed without getting our balls ripped off by the guys at the precinct?"

"Roy Durant told me that other people in the building will be acting funny too, so I vote we do a few more interviews and see what they say."

"Okay, and we can always say we're looking for information about the assault, if the guys ask us about it. I don't want to be the one to tell them that we're investigating reports of an invisible evil darkness taking over Gainsford House and making the residents go crazy."

"Neither do I," Angelo snickered. "We have to talk to the guy from the video of the alleyway, so we might as well ask them about him while we're there. Did anything come up in his background check?"

"No. He seems to be your average law abiding nice guy," Ray replied as he took the document from his jacket pocket and read it. "Works for a successful advertising company and is one of their top guys. He's an only child, parents are still alive and living in Wisconsin, was well educated and seems to be doing well for himself. No significant other at the moment and apart from a couple of parking tickets, he's clean."

"Apart from he gets his kicks by jacking off at murder scenes," Angelo said.

"Yeah, apart from that."

"This makes me scared y'know, if and when my wife and I ever have daughters."

"I know what you mean. You can never know if someone is a deviant. They can be the picture of respectability on the outside, just the type you want your daughters to be with, and they're hiding this sort of thing. It's creepy. If I ever have daughters, I'll try to encourage them to become nuns." Angelo laughed and nodded.

Harlon stood in his kitchen at three in the morning and looked around. He recognised it as his own, but his emotional connection with it had disappeared. It was now nothing more than shelter from the elements and a place in which to secure the opening of the portal in safety. It was still essentially Harlon that stood waiting for the coffee to brew, but he was different now. The controlling force that drove him allowed enough of his own self through so he could take care of his physical body. Being of the physical world, It knew that the Portal Keeper had certain needs, and in order for him to maintain the opening of the portal, he needed to be in good physical shape. He was himself enough to eat, drink, wash, sleep, shit, and make conversation with others if it could not be avoided, but everything else that made Harlon unique was stored away deep inside. There was no ambition, no dreams of the future, no regrets from the past, and no emotion of any kind anymore. One single purpose defined his continued existence now, opening the portal.

No dreams filled Harlon's sleep, he spent the hours within a dark void that did not refresh his mind, and awoke at eleven thirty, his head heavy and throbbing. After showering, dressing, and eating, he sat down and waited for the controlling force to give orders. No television entertained him during the hours of the day, and no music beat throbbed through the apartment. Silence kept him company as he waited patiently. Twice he got up to pee, make coffee and at three in the afternoon, he made himself a sandwich, which he ate in silence. It took several seconds before the chimes of the doorbell worked their way through the empty void of Harlon's mind to the controlling force within. Getting up stiffly, he walked down the hall and opened the door.

"Mr Harlon Drake?"

"Yes."

"Detectives Lamora and Stellman," Angelo said as they held up their badges. "We need to ask you a few questions. May we come in?"

Harlon checked each badge in turn, the effort of using his own mind almost too great. All the time the controlling force was overseeing everything, giving the orders as to how he was to reply and react, and the result was difficult, clumsy, and unnatural. In order for Harlon to react naturally, It had to concede a little control over his mind, which meant there was the real possibility that he could try to regain control over himself. This had to be avoided at all costs, the success of Its mission still depended upon Harlon being compliant, so It had to maintain enough control of him to avoid the possibility. Consequently, his reactions were slow, and the detectives noticed right away.

"Yes, come in," Harlon finally replied and stood aside to let them in. Angelo and Ray entered the hall and watched as he shut the door behind them, then turned around and looked at them expectantly.

"This might take some time, Mr Drake," Ray said. "Should we perhaps sit down and be comfortable?"

Another couple of seconds passed as Harlon and the controlling force computed this request, before he nodded and led the way through to the sitting room and sat down without offering the detectives a seat. They sat down anyway, after exchanging surprised looks.

"Mr Drake," Angelo began. "Can you tell me what you were doing at one seventeen yesterday afternoon?"

"I was here all day," Harlon replied after another couple of seconds, during which his face remained blank and expressionless.

"Did you leave your apartment at all during the day?" Ray asked.

"I went out to the store sometime during the morning, but I felt ill and came home without having purchased anything."

"And did you go out at any other time during the day?" Angelo pushed.

"I did try to go out again later on," Harlon admitted, "but I can't say exactly what time it was. "I hadn't managed to make it to the store earlier, so when I thought I felt better, I tried again."

"Where did you go that second time?" Ray said.

"I only made it a couple of blocks south before I felt sick. I found an alleyway and spent a few minutes there until my stomach settled, before coming home again."

"And what did you do while you were in the alley Mr Drake?" Angelo continued.

Several seconds of silence ensued, during which Harlon locked eyes with Angelo, and the detective would swear for the rest of his life that what looked back at him was not quite human. That expression chilled him and he took comfort in the knowledge that his partner was right beside him.

"I masturbated," Harlon replied, the matter of fact tone surprising both detectives. "Is that a crime?"

"Yes, Mr Drake, I'm afraid it is. You can't do that in a public place in New York."

"I'm sorry, it won't happen again."

"Why did you do it?" Ray asked.

"My head was throbbing, and it sometimes eases a headache. I was worried about getting home without being sick in public and thought if I eased my headache I might make it home safely."

Angelo and Ray were stumped. Both being healthy males, they knew the effect that masturbation had on the body and had used it themselves on occasion to relax.

"Has someone complained?" Harlon asked.

"No, but the security video cameras in the alleyway filmed your visit."

"Then could I apologise to the companies involved? Would that help this situation?"

"I'll tell you what," Angelo said. "I'll talk to the companies that saw the video and see what they say. If they're happy to let this drop with a written apology, then so be it, but you must be aware that they may wish to proceed with a formal complaint."

"Thank you and I can assure you it won't happen again."

"Okay," Ray nodded. "Now can we ask you about something else while we're here?"

"Of course," Harlon replied as his lips drew back from his teeth, and Angelo could not decide whether he was smiling or grimacing. It must be a smile, he decided, even though it did not touch his eyes.

"Have you noticed anything strange going on in Gainsford House lately?"

"You mean apart from a gruesome murder and an intruder?"

"Yeah, apart from that. Anything weird that you can't explain properly? Any uneasiness about the place maybe."

Another of those uneasy silent moments settled over them as Harlon locked eyes, this time with Ray, his vacant stare scaring the shit out of the detective.

"No, I can't say I've noticed anything like that, Detective. Can you be more specific?"

"Just weird or strange," Ray replied. "Maybe a sense that something is lurking in the shadows, a feeling of being watched perhaps."

"No, nothing like that," Harlon replied. "Do you wish me to call you if I do?"

"Yes please," Angelo said, putting his card on the coffee table. "Here's my number if you need to call me." He stood, motioning for Ray that the interview was over, and they headed for the door, Harlon's vacuous stare burning into his back and creeping him out. They entered the corridor and turned to thank Harlon, but the door clicked shut before either of them spoke.

Angelo leaned against the wall behind them. "Oh shit what a creepy dude."

"That is one fucked up guy," Ray said as he ran a hand through his hair. "The way he looked at me was weird. Like something out of a horror movie."

"Yeah, tell me about it. I'm so glad to be out of there."

"Let's see what the other residents think of him huh? Maybe we'll learn something interesting."

15

It rested in its own dimension on the other side of the portal. Until the seeds of influence had percolated throughout the building and exercised a measure of control over the emotions of the residents, It still needed respite in a familiar and safe domain. The malodorous taint of love for life was still strong enough to do serious damage; safety demanded that no risks be taken by remaining too long outside safe harbour. Once the residents were safely under a measure of influence, and were providing enough negative energy, It could remain in the physical world for longer periods. Eventually It would be able to remain indefinitely if the humans provided the right kind of energetic fuel in the right quantity. When that time came, the Portal Keeper would not be needed, but until then, it was necessary to ensure his compliance.

From time to time, It became aware of the Portal Keeper trying to fight back from the confines of his mind, and firmly thrust him back under control. It knew that now he was aware of the plan, he could be a liability if he got away from Its control. He was allowed to tend to his own physical needs in order to keep him healthy enough to do Its bidding, and so as not to raise suspicion amongst his fellow humans. Beyond that, It kept him in a state of torpor. Neither asleep nor awake and functioning independently either. He was kept under tight restraint until It became aware of other humans approaching and seeking interaction from him.

Gradually, It awakened him enough so that he could interact with his fellow humans, but not enough that he could speak of his own free will. It allowed him to interact with the two male humans detected through his physical senses. These two had influence over other humans, and from their questioning of him, the Portal Keeper seemed to have offended his peers in some way. These two strangers were in a position to punish him, and whilst the laws of the physical human world were of no consequence to It, the Portal Keeper still was. It had no choice but to loosen the ties with which he was bound, in order for him to communicate appropriately and with enough emotion to make his contrition seem genuine. This meant that there was a serious risk of him breaking free and saying something to his fellows that might raise their curiosity too high. It used as much control as was possible and prepared to use the Portal Keeper to deal with them if they became a threat.

Once he was alone, It put him back into a deep meditative state until he was needed to open the portal again. It required a lot of energy to exercise enough control of him, and until he had become properly melded with his controller, he would always be at risk of fighting back if It lessened the hold too far. If the Portal Keeper proved useful and trustworthy, It would keep him alive as a useful bridge between It and the human world. There were times when human senses and physical abilities were useful, and being a purely energetic being meant that It had no voice of its own, nor any means of physically interacting with the humans. It exerted influence on inanimate objects easily enough, as with the knives used on the man who loved to kill, but sometimes another human voice or physical body could be of great benefit. It knew that the longer the Portal Keeper's mind remained under control, the more he would lose his own identity and eventually become a living embodiment of It, with Its thoughts, Its drives, and Its plan foremost in his mind. Being physical meant that he was vulnerable to damage though, and until he was no longer needed to open the portal, he must be kept safe from harm. After that, he could prove himself useful or become energetic fuel himself.

16

Up on the fourteenth floor, classical music filtered through apartment eighty. Nessy Bellinger found light classics restful, and often used it to calm her mind and relieve the stress. This was usually at the end of a working day, after being forced into close contact with people on the train both to and from work. The chaos of their energies and their often frantic deceased relatives would almost drive her mad. Today, Nessy wanted the music to help calm her mind away from the dreadful sense of impending doom that seemed to ooze from the building. Her spirit friend Patty had already warned her to get stocked up with supplies and remain inside her apartment until further notice, so Nessy had taken a couple of weeks of her remaining holiday from her work, and shopped like she had never shopped before.

Boxes of cans and cartons now stood stacked against the wall in the spare bedroom, and her freezer bulged at the seams with anything likely to go off quickly. She could remain inside her apartment without suffering hardship for more than three weeks at least. Patty had assured Nessy that steps were being taken to ensure that whatever was happening in Gainsford House would not find her, so long as she remained within the confines of her own apartment. Nessy promised, for she trusted Patty, and when the spirit woman had made her promise to obey without question, she had not hesitated to give her word. She sat and relaxed, for she knew that before too many more days had passed, she would be required to act to save Gainsford House and its residents. She had no idea what would be asked of her, but she made the decision that whatever it was, she would do her best and not hesitate. This was probably the reason she had been burdened with this gift, she surmised.

Angelo and Ray exchanged a glance. They had spent several hours interviewing many of Gainsford House's residents, and had learned that Harlon Drake was a thoroughly nice person who always helped when he was able, had never offended anyone, was always friendly and talkative, and was the kind of person everyone would be happy to introduce to their mother.

"This doesn't sound like the way I would describe the guy we saw earlier today," Angelo said.

"I know. It's like they're talking about a different guy."

"Well either everyone is lying, or there's another Harlon Drake living here, or his demeanour is a recent development."

"We know he's the only Harlon Drake, so that's out and I doubt the whole building would lie about him. A few maybe could be persuaded to lie, but a whole building of people? No way."

"Then he's changed recently."

"And that begs the question why has he changed."

"A black curse from hell perhaps" Angelo offered and Ray grinned.

"Shame Mrs Hanny wasn't at home. We have to come back and interview her again. I'd be interested in what she has to say about what's going on here."

Angelo nodded. "Yeah. The concierge said she'll be," he began but shouts cut him off. Both detectives looked towards the entrance door of Gainsford House, and the busy street outside where a crowd was gathered, the screams of several women reaching their ears. As one, they rushed for the door and out into the warm evening.

The crowd parted at their yells, glad to know that a police officer would now take care of this horror. The remains lay on the sidewalk, a large pool of blood rapidly heading towards the gutter. The head had cracked like an egg. The contents spilled onto the sidewalk, a macabre version of the artworks displayed in city centres by talented artists with nothing more than chalk and imagination. As Angelo looked at it, he noticed the legs and arms lying in positions so strange that the body appeared less human and more like some kind of nightmarish creation dreamed up by a horror movie director. He was surprised at the lack of obvious gore; he would expect there to be gallons of blood and lumps of brain matter scattered for metres around, but the remains held on to their contents surprisingly well. Bystanders stood with hands over their mouths, shocked into silence and unable to tear their gaze away. A father tried to shield his young child from the sight, despite the child trying its best to get a better look. His youthful curiosity was thankfully blocking him from a lifetime of mental harm from having witnessed it. Women cried, and one still screamed as she looked fearfully at the spatters of blood that tainted her ankles, too afraid to wipe them off.

"Come on with me precious," a female voice from Angelo's left said. "Come with me and let's clean you up huh?" He saw the female concierge from Gainsford House who was on the twilight shift. He nodded his thanks to her and allowed her to steer the still crying woman away.

Ray pointed up and Angelo craned his neck. "We'll need the numbers of all apartments with windows on this side of the building. I reckon that's two per floor. That makes forty four doors to knock."

"I think we can safely rule out everything on the first five or six floors," Angelo replied. "Those kind of injuries need quite a height."

Ray nodded. "Okay, let's see if she has any ID on her."

The body was dressed in a floral cotton nightdress, and appeared middle aged to the detectives.

Angelo pointed to the arms. "See the elbows? They show a person's age quicker than anything else. See these are a little wrinkled? I reckon she's in her forties at least."

"She's someone's mom." Ray indicated a necklace around the neck, resting in the pool of blood. Angelo saw a gold heart with something engraved upon it. Ray wiped the blood away with a gloved finger. 'I love my mom' was emblazoned across it.

"It could mean her mom," Angelo said suddenly.

Ray nodded and stood as the sound of sirens came to his ears. "The team has arrived. They stood, both looking towards the sound.

Twenty minutes later, the two detectives stood at the concierge's desk, the woman having now returned to her duty after handing over care of the woman to another police officer.

Angelo smiled at the dumpy redhead with the friendly face. "Thank you. You did good."

She gave a weak smile. "No problem. I used to work with a volunteer crisis response group, and my old job as counsellor comes in handy sometimes."

"I don't suppose you recognise the victim?" Ray asked.

"Sorry. I couldn't get close enough to recognise her." The detectives nodded.

"No problem," Angelo said. "We need to find out which apartment she fell from, so can you give us the numbers of all the ones that have windows looking out over the front of the building?"

"Sure thing." She tapped at her computer. A diagram of the building popped up, and she wrote down a list of numbers. "There you are." She handed the paper to Angelo.

"Which of these apartments has a middle aged woman either living there or visiting?" Ray asked.

The concierge opened a file and scanned down the list, crossing off a good number. When she finished, the detectives had a slightly smaller list of numbers to deal with. Instead of forty-four apartments to check, they now had thirty-one. They also had the names of all the residents in those thirty-one apartments.

"I vote we start from the top and work down," Ray said and Angelo nodded.

Angelo yawned as he knocked on the door of apartment ninety-four on the sixteenth floor, home of Mr David Walldike and his wife, Connie Walldike. They were about to assume the couple were not at home, when the door opened and a scowling man regarded them.

"Yes?"

"Mr David Walldike?" Angelo asked.

"Yes."

"I'm detective Lamora and this is my partner, detective Stellman. Is your wife at home?"

"My wife?"

"Yes. Your wife. Can we speak to her?"

"She's not at home, sorry." He went to shut the door but Ray quickly stuck his foot in the gap.

"What happened to her, Mr Walldike?"

The man stared into Ray's eyes before opening the door wide. "She nagged me."

"She nagged you?" Angelo asked, not able to keep the note of incredulity from his voice. "So you pushed her out the window?"

"Yes. She nagged me and wouldn't shut up. Now she's quiet and won't nag me again."

Ray and Angelo exchanged disbelieving glances, before arresting him for murder.

Once another officer had taken Mr Walldike away to the precinct, Angelo and Ray sat on the stairs between floor sixteen and floor fifteen and talked about the recent events that had taken place at Gainsford House. Both knew that something extremely weird was happening, but neither of them could fathom what, or why.

"Y'know," Ray said. "I'm kind of embarrassed to admit it, but I'm not so sure we should dismiss Mrs Hanny and her evil curse from hell so readily."

"Me neither. We might as well pay her a visit while we're here."

Apartment forty-eight was furnished in a busy fashion. Heavy floral curtains hung at the windows, and matching cushions lay on the dark green sofa on which a large hairy cat slept.

"That's Sekhmet, she won't harm you. Sit down please, would you like some herb tea?"

"Sekhmet?" Ray asked. "That's an unusual name for a cat."

"She was an Egyptian lioness headed goddess, the protector of the pharaohs."

"Interesting," he lied.

"Tea?"

"Do you have coffee?" Angelo asked.

"I have instant, if that's okay."

"That'll be fine, thank you. Do you happen to be friends with Mr and Mrs Walldike from number ninety four?"

"Walldike?" Mrs Hanny frowned. "The name doesn't ring a bell. Why do you ask?"

"We're trying to find out as much as we can about the couple," Ray said as he shot Angelo a glance. "Mr Walldike murdered his wife a few minutes ago."

Mrs Hanny's eyes widened as her mouth opened in shock. She stared at the detectives for long moments before speaking. "Did he do it here in the building?" Ray nodded. "Oh not again."

"What do you mean, again?" Angelo said.

"Another moment of evil here in this building. Think back over the last few days, how many moments of evil have happened here? This makes it six so far. How often do six bad things happen in the same building? Well, how many?"

"Not often at all," Angelo replied. "What do you think is happening here?"

"I don't know. Whatever it is though, it's based in evil, that I can tell you."

"How can you be so sure?" Ray asked.

"Because the people who live in this building are changing."

"Changing? How?"

"People think I'm just a daft old woman. I'm that crazy old bird with silly ideas, and maybe they're right, but I keep my eyes and ears wide open,

Officers. I know most of what goes on in this building, not because I'm nosey. Well I might be a little." She gave an embarrassed laugh. "No, I keep abreast of what happens here because I live here, and the energy of a place is important when you spend the majority of your time there. Negative energy has a negative effect, whereas positive energy enhances your life. The energy comes from people mostly, and when the energy they give off changes, I want to know about it as soon as possible so that if it becomes too bad, I can move out before it affects my life in a detrimental way."

"Sounds sensible to me," Angelo said and Ray nodded enthusiastically. "I take it the energy here is changing in a bad way?" Mrs Hanny nodded. "Can you explain it to us a little more? It might help us deal with the serious crimes that have been committed here."

"It started about a week ago. Gainsford House has always been a wonderful place to live, calm and peaceful. Then suddenly, the place felt spooky. Like there was something dark in the atmosphere when I came home from shopping and rode the elevator. It got stronger the higher the elevator went, and when I got out on the eighth floor I knew it was coming from somewhere above me. I've seen nice, kind, loving people, turn into cold-hearted soulless husks in days. People who used to smile and speak to me now refuse to acknowledge me and their eyes are dead looking. I'm scared, I don't mind admitting it, and I've decided to sell up and move out."

Angelo and Ray looked at each other when Mrs Hanny mentioned dead eyes, and both knew the other was thinking of Harlon Drake. She could easily have been describing him, and both registered a chill flutter into life deep within.

"I know it sounds silly Mrs Hanny," Angelo said, "but how would you suggest my partner and I handle this umm, darkness?"

"By not handling it at all. I would suggest you leave this building and never return. Whatever this is, it's way too big for us ordinary humans to handle. We have to let it work itself out and hope higher realms do something."

"Higher realms?" Ray asked with a frown.

"The higher spirit realms. The higher realms of the spirit world are inhabited by highly evolved spirit beings, and only they have the knowledge and power to go into battle with whatever this is here."

"How do you know all this Mrs Hanny?" Angelo asked.

"Sekhmet tells me."

"The cat?"

"Yes."

"You talk to your cat?"

"Yes. We communicate telepathically."

"Does she know anything about Harlon Drake from the twelfth floor?" Ray shrugged when Angelo glared at him.

"As a matter of fact I know him. Only by having exchanged conversation in the elevator though. Funny you should ask about him."

"Oh?"

"He's one of the ones who has changed the most. I saw him in the elevator yesterday and I was so unsettled that I got out on the second floor and caught the other elevator."

"In what way would you say he's changed?" Angelo said.

"He used to be friendly. He smiled readily when he spoke to you and made you feel he was genuinely interested in you. When I saw him yesterday, it was as if his soul had gone from within his body. I know it sounds crazy but it was creepy as hell. I had to get away from him. As soon as I got back here I felt compelled to cleanse the whole apartment and myself too."

"It doesn't sound crazy to us Mrs Hanny," Angelo assured her. "Not crazy at all."

"Would you like me to call you when something else happens here?"

"Oh that would be most helpful," Ray said, handing over his card.

By the time both detectives left Gainsford House, they had eaten delicious ham sandwiches, coffee cake, drank more coffee, and graciously subjected themselves to a cleansing from Mrs Hanny. Their clothes smelled strongly of sage, and both knew that the guys back at the precinct would tease them about it for ages, but they did not care. Angelo was scared to admit to Ray that the cleansing smoke administered by the expert hands of Mrs Hanny had made his headache go away. He had no way of knowing, but Ray was also pleased to have submitted to the old woman's ministrations, for his growing irritation with Angelo and his greater popularity with their peers quickly vanished. Once out in the fresh night air, both took several seconds to breathe deeply.

"I think we spent too long inside the building tonight," Ray said.

"Huh?"

"I vote we keep our visits here to a minimum. The longer we spend in there, the more it affects us. Didn't you feel it?"

"What?"

"I can't explain it," Ray said. "I just know that a couple of minutes outside here in the fresh air and it's like I've woken up from a half sleep or something. I know you felt it too. I saw you rub your temples a few times."

"I did have a headache. Mrs Hanny and her smoke got rid of it though. It may be all a load of nonsense, but it sure shifted that headache. My head is clearer out here."

"Maybe it's fumes or something natural like that," Ray suggested. "We should get someone to check out whether there's a cracked gas pipe or some weird natural gas seeping from underground."

"Now that's an idea," Angelo nodded. "It's happened before, and gases can make people act funny. Let's get someone out to check for any strange fumes."

"It certainly couldn't hurt."

17

Harlon spent the entire afternoon sitting quietly in his sitting room. The only time he moved was when the two detectives arrived to interview him. Other than that, he only got up or moved at all when he went for a pee, or to make food. At all other times, the thing that controlled his mind kept him in a state much like that of meditation. Inside a dark corner of his mind, his consciousness was aware of everything that happened, and scream as he might, he could not make himself heard. It was only during the interview with the detectives that he was able to influence his body at all, and made his mouth hesitate a little longer than normal before it spoke. He tried desperately to get his body to obey his will, to make it ask for help, and he even tried to get it to attack them so they would arrest him and take him away from Gainsford House. Harlon knew the force that controlled him could not survive away from this building at the moment, and had hoped the detectives might take him away for masturbating in the alleyway. Shame flooded through his mind but even though he owned up to it, they refused to arrest him, and Harlon's soul cried with frustration.

It was as if his mind and his body were two separate and different entities now, instead of one united force, a single entity. When the controller directed him, he was powerless to stop his body from rising from the chair and walking out into the hallway. Opening the door to the Psychomanteum, Harlon switched on the light and sat in the chair. A few days previously, he had been so excited at the prospect of this new experience, and hoped to communicate with the spirit of his dead ancestor. Now he wished with all of his might that he had not dabbled in this business, that he had not heard of Jonathan Rink-Standen. One thing he was sure of though was that in order for the mirror to do its thing, he needed to meditate and concentrate. Guessing that whatever it was that controlled him could not use the mirror without him, Harlon decided to keep his mind busy and active, to prevent the mirror from working.

First, he tried occupying his mind by singing to himself, but that soon became strangely meditative, the repetition serving as a mantra and calming his mind too much. Next he tried counting, first in threes, then fours, then fives, and so on, but that too soon became almost chant like and lulled him into meditation. Then he tried fighting against the controlling force, but that quickly tired him, which made his mind even easier to penetrate and control. Panic approached and stood at the edge of his consciousness, but then a voice caught his attention.

"Hello Harlon, I'm so happy to meet you at last. Please don't be afraid, you will not be hurt."

"What the fuck?" Harlon thought from inside his prison. "Who the fuck is that? Why are you doing this to me?"

"You don't recognise me? After holding me in your heart for so long, you don't know me when I speak? I am Patricia, the forebear of whom you have wondered so often. It is quiet in here and I can approach you and make you hear me."

"Patricia? But why are you doing this? What has happened to my mind, and why can't I control my body anymore. It's like there are two people inside me now, and the wrong one is stronger. Please help me."

"I have been trying to awaken you to a wonderful new experience but you've been resisting me. This is the only way I could think of to reach you and assure you that there is nothing to fear, and that if you go with it, you will be amazed at what is to come."

"But I don't understand. What new experience?"

"You Harlon, because of your inheritance of my unique abilities, are the first of my descendants to inherit the right form of the ability that enables you to reach me in the way I am going to teach you. Few people from your physical world have this ability, and what you will experience is like nothing you could imagine. You must trust me though, and not resist anymore. Unless of course you wish not to communicate with me anymore. That is your right of course. I will withdraw and never communicate with you again. I will not force the gift upon you."

"No, wait, don't go," Harlon replied. "I umm, I didn't know what was happening and I got scared. I've never experienced anything like this before and it's natural that I'm going to be a little alarmed huh?" He gave a small nervous laugh. "So it's been you all along, trying to communicate with me and teach me some new communication technique?"

"Yes."

"Was that what made me so ill yesterday whenever I went out among people?"

"Yes, that is a side effect of your changing energies, but it will diminish as you grow used to it. Your physical body will react in all sorts of ways until it gets used to the different energy frequency your astral body will be vibrating at."

"I thought that it was something bad, what with the things that have been going on around here lately. I was so worried when I suddenly felt like someone else was inside my mind and controlling my body. What about the girl I saw murdered, the one in the alleyway, why show me that?"

"That was a hallucination caused by your own subconscious mind. At present, it is struggling to cope with the higher energy frequencies given off by your astral body as you connect with me slightly beyond the physical realm you dwell in. There will be more such sights for you for a while, until your physical body and your astral body regain their balance with each other at the new higher frequency. You must be patient and trust me."

"Thank you and I'm sorry for being so difficult. I'm so happy to know that you have continued after your physical body died. Can I ask you something?"

"You want to know if it hurt when my body died?"

"Yes. I'm sorry if it's too personal, but no one ever found out who killed you or how it happened. It's been a mystery and I always wanted to solve it, as much for you as for anyone else."

"Around the time when I was staying at the Rink-Standen mansion which stood on the site of this building, there had been a series of murders in the vicinity stretching back eighteen months. I was one of his victims, and it wasn't until another four after me were killed, that he was finally killed himself, in the basement of the Rink-Standen mansion itself."

"Who was he?"

"His name was Edward Buck, and he was a neighbour of Jonathan Rink-Standen."

"So what happened?"

"Jonathan was woken one night by the sounds of a commotion coming from his basement, and went to investigate. He found Edward Buck hiding there, claiming to have been framed for murder by two men he had won a large amount of money from in a card game."

"But that wasn't true?"

"No. He begged Jonathan to hide him, but the police turned up a while later and told him Edward had been discovered in the process of abusing and murdering a local girl of fourteen, and was on the run."

"Holy shit. Oh I'm sorry, forgive my language."

"No matter. The police were advising everyone in the neighbourhood to lock their doors and stay inside. Jonathan, being an honest man, told them right away that Edward was hiding in the basement, and they went down to arrest him. There was a scuffle and he fell and impaled his head on a spike from a broken piece of iron railing."

"How did he kill you, and why?"

"He had been one of the guests at one of Jonathan's regular parties, and I met him there. It was obvious right away that he was enamoured of me, but I did not return his feelings. He was married, and not someone that I was attracted to anyway. One night, I was taking a walk in the garden during one of Jonathan's parties before retiring for the night, when he came up behind me, knocking me almost senseless. After forcing himself upon me, he strangled me and left me there. Jonathan's butler found me the next morning."

"Oh I'm so sorry," Harlon said, the emotion clear in his voice.

"It is long ago now, forgotten. Such concerns are of the physical world. Here in the spiritual world we have no cares. There was but a moment of discomfort before I awoke in this new and fabulous realm. Death of the physical body is not the end, but the beginning of something so wonderful you cannot imagine it."

"Thank you for sharing that with me. Now, what do you want me to do?"

"I want you to trust me, to let me guide you, and not to worry about the strange effects this new change is having upon your physical senses. They will go as your body balances with its astral counterpart."

"Okay, now I know it is you, and why you're doing it, I feel so much better. I will do as you ask."

"At this early stage, I can only communicate with you and help you with this development while you're here keeping the portal open."

"The portal?" Harlon asked.

"The mirror. It is a portal that allows me through so I can communicate with you far more easily than any other way. If I have to manifest by your bedside, it will use so much energy that I will have nothing left with which to affect the changes necessary to your energy frequency. That way we will never get to our goal."

"I see. That makes sense. Okay, I will use the mirror whenever you wish me to. How will I know?"

"You will know. I will give you a sudden strong desire to stop whatever you're doing and use the mirror right away. Whenever you notice the compulsion to sit here, don't resist it. Come here right away and open the portal."

"Okay."

"Now I'm going to step aside from your mind. You might be a little dizzy for a while, but don't worry. Sit here and open the portal and by the time we finish for the evening, you will be back to your normal self again."

Harlon relaxed inside his own mind, and all at once felt his consciousness rush outward in all directions, like an explosion within his own mind. For a moment, he feared his physical body would expand with the impact, that it might hurt when the two crashed together, but as soon as his mind registered what was happening, all was still and calm. Looking down at his fingers, he wriggled them and grinned, wriggled his toes inside his socks, got up and stretched his legs before sitting down again as a wave of nausea overcame him. He groaned and closed his eyes.

When his mind calmed, Harlon gazed into the mirror and willed his mind to relax. Within a few minutes, a smoky haze was whirling around the room, around him, but he did not worry this time, for he trusted Patricia implicitly. There was no flight around the building this time, no scenes of horror that worried but excited him so. Strange things had occurred in the building lately, of that Harlon was in no doubt. Doug Morrison's intruder, the killing of Saul Benedict, and the death of the girl in the alleyway a block south, he knew those things had happened, but no longer worried about them. Memories of his initial excitement at the prospect of using the mirror as a Psychomanteum returned to his mind, and he grinned.

It did not seem long before Harlon heard Patricia's voice inside his head again. An involuntary smile spread across his face as he listened to her, delighted at the easy way they were communicating now, and excited at the promise of some new and amazing way of communicating that was to come. He felt honoured to have inherited this special gift from her, and his explorer's nature welled up at the prospect of some new spiritual adventure.

PSYCHOMANTEUM

"You have done well Harlon, and I am so proud to be working with you at last. Feed your body now, then sleep and awake refreshed in the morning. You might find that you are tired tomorrow, so sleep whenever you feel the need and have a quiet day while your body gets accustomed to the changes it's going through. We will talk again tomorrow evening and work some more."

The smoky haze flowed back into the mirror and Harlon was once again alone within the tiny closet that had become the centre of his existence so quickly. With a grin splitting his face in half, he got up and went into the kitchen to make something to eat. It was odd to be fully in charge of his own body again, and it was strangely heavy and lumbering as he plodded across the floor. He had always prided himself on being fit and healthy, but now he felt like an ungainly hippo. With a determined nod, he resolved to lose a few pounds and resume a fitness regimen.

It was wonderful to be fully in charge of himself again, and he indulged in a long hot soak instead of his usual efficient but short shower. His physical senses seemed on high alert, and his body responded quickly to his relaxed state of mind. Long slow and unhurried strokes, aided by the hot water, brought him to a strong climax that almost sent him to sleep right there in the bath. Not wishing to drown, he dragged himself out, wrapped a towelling robe around his body, before padding through to the bedroom and sitting on the edge of the bed. Four hours later he awoke, his body having slipped sideways onto the floor as it fell asleep. Wincing in pain from the hard floor, he stretched, discarded the robe, and slipped into bed. Dreams swamped his mind and he found himself flying through the air, watching his neighbours go about their daily lives, and right before he awoke, he stood atop the highest point of the building and gazed up at the night sky. He knew that somewhere up there, another realm awaited him, a realm few living people got to see, and he was immensely proud.

18

It awoke sharply from slumber, sensing strangers around the Portal Keeper, and focussed towards his mind. This Portal Keeper was new to this level of control and it took a second or two for his body to obey Its orders. In order for the man to interact with his fellows naturally, It needed to loosen control of him a little, but this gave him more room to fight back, and he did. It was far stronger of course, but the Portal Keeper might say something to arouse his companions' suspicions, which could make things awkward. It sensed that the two strangers were in a position of some authority over others of their kind, and therefore could conceivably take the Portal Keeper away against his will. If that happened, all would be lost, for It still needed him to open the portal. A day or two more and he would no longer be necessary, but until then, It must be careful.

Once the immediate threat was over, It probed the Portal Keeper's memory banks for anything to use as leverage. Within minutes, a strong emotional connection between the Portal Keeper and an ancestor named Patricia Drake became apparent. As It dwelt upon this new name, a memory stirred and eventually rose to the surface. Long ago, on the same spot this building now stands upon, a man with deliciously negative energy took the young woman's energy from her physical body. It was shortly before the previous Portal Keeper fought off Its advances and escaped. The young woman's energy was the most vital and strong It had ever tasted. How perfect that this new Portal Keeper should be of her lineage.

It probed Harlon's memories for information with which to weave a lie so convincing that he would never suspect. Knowing that he was desperate for contact with the soul of the woman named Patricia, It surmised that he would do anything she were to ask of him, so long as the reward for his compliance was the promise of further communications with her. This was so easy it was ridiculous, It thought whilst gathering the information together and preparing to begin. With some difficulty, It steered Harlon into the Psychomanteum, but he resisted opening the portal. He must know that It needed him to do it and was using this as a way to fight back. This was the one thing that could not be forced upon him, so It brought forth the lie so expertly created that Harlon was bound to believe it without question.

Once he was compliant, It withdrew from his mind and gathered itself for the night's foray. Having already seeded the building with extremely negative energy, It found this new domain already much more comfortable. The residents within were already changing, becoming living fuel factories for Its continued existence. It drank in the negative energies and flew throughout the building. The stronger It became, the more the residents could be influenced to embrace the comforting darkness of negativity. They succumbed easily, human nature making them only too willing soldiers of this new dark master.

In one apartment, It sensed two people who were still resisting, so concentrated focus on them and watched as the man, suddenly oblivious to the woman's persistent nagging, got up from his chair and approached her. Taking her by the shoulders, he shoved her roughly towards the open window, where she banged her head on the glass. This momentary lapse of concentration on her part, gave the man a window of opportunity that he used to grab her by the legs and upend her out of the window. Her scream cut off suddenly and was followed by others from below, surprised by the manner of her appearance into their lives. Relieved at the quiet, the man shut the window, sat down, and waited to be told what to do.

It sensed the same two strangers from earlier were still in the building and followed them for a while, trying to influence them with strongly negative energy. Their energies were equally strong, It found, and they could easily cause too much of a nuisance. It decided they needed to be dealt with before that happened.

19

Abraham Goodman entered the elevator and punched the access code for the penthouse apartment. It had been a stressful day, made worse by the resignation of an important board member, and by his beautiful and sexually complicit secretary being on holiday. His head ached and without his usual lunchtime fellatio, he was irritable and short tempered. He would have to make do with sex with Cecilia tonight, which was boring at the best of times. There was no way she would suck him like Laura did. The one and only time he had asked his wife for fellatio, she had almost slapped him for his impudence. How he wished she would run off with the butler or something. He had hired a string of young and good-looking butlers during the past five years in the hope that one of them would take her off his hands, but so far, all of them were too intelligent to make such a mistake.

Gabe, the current butler, obviously fancied Cecilia, of that Abraham was sure. He recognised lust in a man's eyes easily, and had dropped a few hints that his wife might be willing.

"Cecilia has taken to you, Gabe," he would say. "I think she has a soft spot for you, Gabe," was another he used regularly. He knew Gabe was not stupid and would know he was being made an offer, and Abraham prayed he would accept. Even if the man did not run off with her, if he caught them at it, he could divorce her without losing a fortune or his reputation. How often he wished he had made her sign a pre-nuptial agreement before they married.

As the elevator passed floor twenty, Abraham's cell phone beeped. It was Jeff, one of the board members reminding him of the early meeting the next day. The elevator door slid open silently and Abraham stepped out, fumbling for his door key while trying to balance the phone between his shoulder and jaw. Jeff was halfway through telling him about a conversation he overheard between two board members of a rival company, when Abraham got the door opened and entered the spacious apartment. He stepped into the living room and was about to comment to Jeff when he noticed Gabe, naked as the day he was born, standing in the middle of the room. He was gazing down at Cecilia, who was equally naked as she knelt before him and suckled at the most enormous penis Abraham had ever seen.

It was not the fact that his wife was cheating on him with their butler that annoyed Abraham; he had wanted to leave her for ages. No, it was the fact that she was giving him oral sex, and that the butler's penis was so huge that made his cheeks flush with anger. When he had asked her to suck him off, she refused point blank, and made him feel like a dirty old man for having asked. Now here she was enjoying it with their butler, who was hung like a horse. Anger and inadequacy flooded Abraham's heart and he forgot the phone call.

"Cecilia? Gabe? What the hell are you two doing?"

"Are you blind, asshole?" Gabe said between sighs and groans of pleasure. Cecilia made sucking noises with her lips and looked at Abraham, taunting him even more by making loud noises as she sucked and licked.

"Oh yeah, Gabe," she groaned. "Come in my mouth baby and then do me from behind."

Abraham's eyes widened in shock as his mouth flapped in disbelief. Not only was she giving oral sex to their butler after refusing to give it to him all the years of their marriage, but she was also asking him to take her from behind. Abraham had always been turned on by taking a woman on her hands and knees, but Cecilia had tried it once and never repeated the experience, with him anyway. All at once Abraham was consumed with anger and all thoughts of the favour Gabe was doing him went out the window.

"Stop it. Stop it at once. Gabe, you're fired you hear me? And you?" He spat at Cecilia. "I'm divorcing you and you'll get nothing from me, you whore."

Gabe suddenly let out a loud grunt as his body shuddered, and Abraham watched as Cecilia sucked and swallowed greedily.

"Go on, get out," he yelled at the top of his voice, pointing towards the front door.

"Not until I've fucked your wife one more time. Gotta do the job you're unable to do for yourself." He stepped around behind Cecilia, who had dropped onto her hands and knees and waited for him, her ass wiggling in the air provocatively. Abraham's face was purple with shame and rage, and he lunged for Gabe, grabbing him around the neck and sending them both sprawling.

"I said get out," Abraham yelled as he fought with Gabe. Although he was much smaller, the weight of his anger and shame carried him along and he held his own as the naked butler tried to fight back. Having so recently experienced a shattering climax, his strength was sapped and Abraham was getting the upper hand. Suddenly, a red-hot spike of pain drove into his spine and he arched his back and cried out, Gabe forgotten instantly. Another, equally sharp spear of pain drove into him, this time slightly lower than the last, the intensity of it taking his breath away. With a huge effort, he turned over onto his back, the pain unlike anything he had ever experienced. Cecilia stood over him, still naked, her breasts swaying slightly as she moved her arm up and behind. The light from the table lamp glinted from the blade, and Abraham saw the knife in her hand, his blood running down the handle and dripping from her fingers.

"Cecilia, please don't kill me," he gasped as she brought her arm down in a swift arcing movement. Abraham's abdomen exploded in pain, and he was vaguely aware of the metallic taste of blood in his mouth before darkness overcame him. Cecilia laughed and sat back, arching her head back as her cackles filled the room. Gabe looked at Abraham, then back at Cecilia, and could not help but join in with her laughter. Once their laughter was spent, he reached for her breasts, the sight of the blood dripping from her nipples turning him on. Back by the still open doorway to the hall, Abraham's cell phone lay on the floor where he dropped it in his shock.

"Abe? Abe are you okay? Abe? Please answer me or I'm calling the cops."

Angelo and Ray were sitting in their office, discussing their interview with David Walldike. Memories of the interviews they did with the Durants came back to both of their minds as they listened to David Walldike howling for his lost wife and begging for the death penalty. Once they had officially ended the interview, having gained a full confession and some rantings about dark forces at work, Angelo switched off the recorder and leaned forwards.

"Now Mr Walldike, off the record, just between you and us. Tell us what happened."

His story had been almost identical to the Durant's story, and both detectives exchanged regular knowing glances. He told them how some dark force seemed to invade his mind and make him do things he did not want to do, and even though he tried to resist, this dark force was too strong for him.

"Connie was always a talkative woman. She worried about me and like to fuss over me all the time. It was one of the things that I always loved about her, and it had never been a nuisance to me before. I would never want to kill her; I've loved her since I was seventeen."

"But you did kill her last night," Angelo said. David Walldike nodded and burst into tears.

"I know, and I saw myself doing it but couldn't stop myself. I want the death penalty. Please, I want to join Connie."

"Take it easy David," Ray soothed. "Angelo and I want to sort out whatever it is that's going on up at Gainsford House, so that no one else has to go through what you've been through. Anything you tell us now your official interview is over is strictly between us."

He blew his nose and wiped his eyes. "There's something horrible there. Connie mentioned it a day or so before but I blew it off as just her silly imaginings. I wish I'd listened to her now."

"What did she say?" Angelo asked.

"She said the place gave her the creeps. This was something she'd never said before. When we looked over the apartment, the warm feeling was one of the things she mentioned as making her want to buy the place."

"Did she know why it gave her the creeps? Or how?" Ray said.

"All she said was that the shadows in the corners were darker than they used to be, that the corridors were spooky, like monsters were waiting around every corner. She said the place felt evil all of a sudden. I told her she was being silly or having a mid-life crisis. I should've listened to her." He burst into a fresh flood of tears and the detectives handed him a cigarette.

"Anything from the gas guy yet?" Angelo asked.

Ray shook his head. "I did get a call from the store that owns the surveillance camera in the alleyway. They said they can't afford a court case, and as the guy didn't actually hurt anyone, they'd be happy to let it go if he writes them a letter of apology and agrees to keep away from their business."

"Probably the best course of action. What do you think about all this evil spooky shit?"

"Up until now I would never have given such a thought the time of day. Now, after everything that's happened up there, I'm not too sure I can be so dismissive."

"Me neither. What do we do about it?"

Ray shrugged. "Shit, how the fuck do I know? First, we wait for the gas guy to give us his report. There may be some odourless gas seeping up from some deep fault line or something that's giving everyone hallucinations and crazy thoughts. If he says there's nothing there, then, umm, hell I don't know. Consult a priest maybe."

"We could maybe get one of those ghost hunting teams to come out and spend the night in the place. There are a few empty apartments they could hole up in for the night. See what they come up with."

"That's an idea," Ray nodded. "There's that psychic woman that's helped out on that child murder case last year. We could give her a call and see what she says about it."

Angelo nodded. "Yeah, good idea. Y'know, we should have a talk before we spend too much time in there again ourselves."

"Huh?"

"Last night, after we'd spent several hours in the building, we both said the place had started to affect us, remember?" Ray nodded and looked at the floor. "Do you think maybe we should talk about stuff so it can't affect us again? Maybe get anything either of us has been sitting on secretly, out into the open?"

"I guess it wouldn't hurt," Ray replied quietly, obviously uncomfortable.

"I don't want anything between us that could put us against each other if things get worse in there. We're both armed remember? I have a wife and you have your whole life ahead of you."

"Then how about if we leave our guns in the car whenever we go inside the place?" Ray suggested and Angelo nodded.

"It's a good idea in the circumstances, even though it puts both of us at a disadvantage if anyone else should come at us. I'd rather have to fight my way out of a situation than shoot my partner, or have him shoot me."

"Yeah, me too."

"So what do you want to tell me?" Angelo asked.

"Huh?" Ray frowned.

"Any grudges you're holding for me? Anything I do that makes you angry? Have I ever hurt you?" Ray blushed and Angelo knew something was coming. "Come on now, this could save both our lives remember."

"Well it irritates me that you're more popular with the guys than me. It's like I'm your partner, but you're never mine y'know? Like I'm always your sidekick. I work as hard as you do, but you always get everyone's praise and I have to make do with a pat on the back."

"I'm sorry, I didn't know you felt that way," Angelo said, surprised at his partner's confession. "Have I been doing anything to make it worse? Is there any way I can stop it from happening, or at least lessen it a little?"

"You could stop being so competitive with me," Ray replied. Angelo nodded immediately. They had always had a friendly rivalry between them, but it never occurred to him that Ray might be suffering emotionally because of it.

"That's no problem," he said. "I can do that easily. I wish you'd said something before, then it needn't have gone on so long. I'm sorry if I made you feel left behind. I never meant it that way. We've been partners since we joined the force, and I wouldn't want anyone else with me out there. Everything we do, we do together, as a team. Maybe I haven't given you enough confirmation of that though."

"Thanks," Ray nodded and blushed. "What about you? Anything I do that makes you angry?"

"Just one. You always put things off, and that irritates the fuck out of me."

"How do you mean?"

"Not important stuff like reports or anything like that. You're always bang on with everything that matters. No, it's stupid stuff that shouldn't get to me, but I've always been the type of person that gets stuff done and out of the way, and the way you drag your heels over it annoys me no end."

"What sort of stuff?" Ray asked, intrigued.

"For instance, the air con in your car." Ray laughed aloud and nodded. "You could've got that done weeks ago but you left it and left it and still it's not done."

"It's being done Friday."

"I know, but which Friday?" Angelo said. "I will try to relax about it, but being honest here, this does annoy me."

"And if I'm honest, I guess I do sometimes string it out on purpose cos I know it annoys you."

"Really?" Angelo said. Ray nodded. "Wow, I would never have thought that of you."

"I guess it's my way of getting back at you for being Mr Popularity around here. It's childish I guess. Sorry buddy."

"Thanks for being honest, and I forgive you."

"Thanks. I forgive you too." Ray extended his hand and Angelo shook it. Both hoped that there was nothing left lurking in either of their minds that could cause a problem, should things at Gainsford House get worse. Suddenly the phone rang. Ray leaned over and picked it up.

"Detective Stellman." He listened for a moment, before snapping his head up. "Okay, thanks. Keep us informed huh?" He put the phone down.

"Well?" Angelo asked.

"That was the gas guy. He can detect nothing in or around Gainsford House that is a cause for worry. He's taken water samples, in case some kind of hallucinogen has been released into the water supply, and he'll have the results for us in a day or so."

"So whatever it is, it's not something natural that's making folks go nuts up there," Angelo said and ran a hand through his hair.

"Looks like we're back with the black curse from hell," Ray said.

Suddenly the door burst open and Detective Suzy Shields ran in. "Guys, there's been another murder at your favourite place."

PSYCHOMANTEUM

20

Angelo and Ray wasted no time getting to Gainsford House, the report of an injured officer at the scene snapping everyone into emergency mode instantly. Several cars with sirens wailing arrived at the front entrance to the building, with Ray screeching to a halt beside them seconds later. They raced into the building behind the uniformed officers, and Angelo noticed the same female concierge from the day before. She nodded to them and called out the special code that would enable the elevator to go right up to the penthouse apartment. He nodded his thanks and followed the others to the elevator.

The uninjured young officer was waiting for them inside the front door. His partner had received a knife wound to his left bicep, which was deep but no more than a flesh wound. Entering the penthouse, Angelo and Ray took in the scene. The first thing they noticed was a naked woman with wrists and ankles both handcuffed. She writhed on the floor and spat obscenities constantly, her body red with blood. A dead male lay on the floor, bloodstains on his abdomen and back giving away the manner of his death. Another dead body, this time a naked black male lay near the window, a hole in his chest giving testament to one of the officers' marksmanship. A blood-stained knife lay on the floor near his right hand.

"Okay talk to me," Angelo said to the uninjured officer.

"We received a call to come and investigate a possible assault. The white male you see over there, Mr Abraham Goodman, was talking on his cell phone with a colleague as he entered the apartment approximately seventy-three minutes ago. The colleague, a Mr Jeff Randall, heard raised voices, and Mr Goodman telling someone to get out. He then heard Mr Goodman telling his wife that he intended to divorce her. After that, Mr Goodman shouted "Cecilia, please don't kill me." This was followed by a woman's screech and some gurgling noises. Mr Goodman never spoke again, despite Mr Randall spending several minutes on the phone shouting for him to answer. He heard what sounded like a man and woman groaning and deduced that they were having sex, and recognised the woman's voice as Mrs Cecilia Goodman, the woman handcuffed over there. Mr Randall then broke off the call and phoned the police. Hank and I got the call to come and investigate, and when we got here, a black male rushed us and Hank got a flesh wound. I shot him, and Hank and I got Mrs Goodman handcuffed. Due to her aggressive nature, we had to restrain her feet and hands, for our own safety and to prevent her escape."

"Okay, good job. Get back to the precinct and write up your report, we'll take over here. The boss will explain the process you'll go through from here on. Have you ever fired your weapon before?"

"No."

"Okay, don't worry. Just get back to the precinct and write up your report. By the time you're done the Boss will be able to explain things to you. As soon as the medics arrive, we'll get Hank's arm looked at and he'll join you back at base. I'll sort out someone to drive you back."

"Okay."

Angelo and Ray watched as a still fighting and spitting Cecilia Goodman was wrapped in a blanket and led away, then exchanged shocked glances.

"Wow, hell hath no fury like a woman scorned," Angelo said.

"I wonder what her husband did to deserve this end."

"From what we know so far, it seems the wife was having it away with the other guy, and the husband came home and found them together."

Ray nodded. "What do you bet that after a night in a cell, she's full of remorse?"

"Yeah. I wouldn't be at all surprised, and I also bet that at some point, she'll talk about something evil in the building."

Ray nodded. "Can this get any crazier?"

"Who knows?" Angelo stepped aside as a team of medics arrived and crouched down by Hank to check his arm.

"This is becoming a habit," a female voice said. "People will talk if we keep meeting like this."

"Hello again, Doctor Mathers," Angelo said.

"What do you have for me tonight?"

"A black male, shot by an officer, and a white male, stabbed in the back."

"I see the black male is naked," she called from the other side of the room. "What did he do to deserve a shot to the heart?"

"He was attacking an officer with that knife by his right hand," Ray replied, a little annoyed at her remark. Julia Mathers nodded. Five minutes later, she picked up her bag.

"Okay, they're all yours. Time of death on the black guy is already known. The white male died within the last couple of hours. Ship them over and I'll do the autopsies tomorrow."

"Okay," Ray nodded. "That fits with the information we have, thanks."

"What is it with this building?" she asked.

"That's what we're trying to find out," Angelo said. "All the residents will tell us is that there is something evil roaming the building."

"Something evil? Are you serious?"

"Yeah I know. Kinda crazy huh?"

"I wouldn't argue with you there," she grinned. "I'll call you when I have the reports."

"Thanks Doc," Angelo said and watched her ass sway as she walked down the hallway and out the door.

"Was she making some kind of statement?" Ray asked.

"What do you mean?"

"When she asked what the black guy did to deserve a shot to the heart. She never asked what the white guy did to deserve a knife in the back."

"That's true. It's probably because she had a mixed race cousin who was shot by a cop."

"Oh?"

"Yeah. One of her mother's sisters married an African American, and one of their kids got in with a gang in Detroit where they lived. The gang was holding up a drug store when the cops were called, and it ended up with him being shot and injured by a cop. He lost a kneecap and almost never walked again."

"Wow, how did you know all this?" Ray asked.

"Ted Fancourt told me. He knew her from years back when she first started working at the Medical Examiner's Office. They dated briefly."

"No wonder I didn't know then. Ted and I don't exactly get on."

"You were in the wrong there y'know," Angelo said. "You should apologise."

"I know, and I tried but he blew me off. You must admit it did look suspicious, especially at first."

"Yeah, but that doesn't mean it was right to make a huge scene about it in front of the other guys. He never did have any affair with that witness; it was proved beyond any doubt."

"I know, and I felt bad about it. It still sort of embarrasses me I guess, and a couple of the guys still mention it from time to time."

"Do they?" Angelo asked.

"Yeah. If I annoy anyone, someone will get sarcastic and mention it. It's what they always use to beat me with, and I gave it to them myself."

"Then if you wait until all the guys are together, before apologising to Ted in front of them all, you'll take the control back from them and regain a lot of respect. Even if he refuses to accept your apology, the fact that you own your mistake and show the balls enough to apologise will make a huge difference."

"Yeah, you may be right," Ray nodded.

Angelo was about to push the point further, but changed his mind when he remembered where they were. He did not want to create any tension between them that could potentially cause a dangerous situation. In their rush to get to the scene and protect their officers, they had both forgotten to leave their guns in the car. This new murder meant the neighbours would have to be interviewed, at least on the floor below, and that meant they would be in the building for a couple of hours without a break.

"I'm with you, whatever you decide okay?"

"Thanks."

With the forensic team arriving, the detectives decided to get on with interviewing the neighbours on the floor below the penthouse.

"You wanna split it?" Ray asked.

"No. With everything that's been going on here, I think we should stick together. We don't know how many other crazy neighbours there are hiding behind those front doors."

"Okay, let's get to it and hope for no more crazies."

"Yep," Angelo agreed. "We have apartments one hundred and twenty seven to one hundred and thirty two. According to the information we got last time we knocked on doors, number one two nine is empty and for sale, Mr Jason Rackman in one thirty is in Europe, and Miss Elly Walker in one thirty two works nights and will be at work by now. That leaves us three interviews."

"You never know," Ray said. "We could find that nobody heard a thing and be out of here within ten minutes and heading to the doughnut shop."

"Let's hope for that huh?" Angelo said as they descended the stairs. With a quick look at Ray, who nodded, he knocked on the door of apartment one twenty seven and waited. The door was yanked open almost immediately, making both detectives jump. Ray's hand instinctively settled on the butt of his gun as it sat against his chest in its holster. A big man glared at them, and Angelo could not help but notice that his biceps were almost the size of his thighs.

"Ain't you those cops that were here asking questions the other day?" a deep voice demanded.

"Yes Sir," Angelo replied, forcing his mouth into something resembling a smile. "We're sorry to bother you again, Mr Mitchell, but there's been an incident upstairs in the penthouse apartment. We have to ask everyone on this floor if they heard anything unusual in the last couple of hours."

"I heard a gunshot a few minutes ago, and what sounded like a woman screaming. What's going on?"

"There's been a murder, Mr Goodman has died," Ray replied.

"Another one? What's happening around here?"

"That's what we're trying to find out," Angelo said. "What can you tell us about the Goodmans?"

"Not much. Mr Goodman is rich, I mean was rich. He worked long hours and must've worked seven days a week as I can't remember the last time he was home for a whole day. The sound carries you see, through the air vents."

"And what about Mrs Goodman?" Ray asked. "What can you tell us about her?"

"Well," the man hesitated and both detectives knew they were going to hear something interesting. "I reckon she was playing away."

"Playing away?" Angelo said with a frown. "You mean she was having an affair?"

"Yeah, with that butler of theirs."

"Oh. What makes you say that?"

"Like I said, the sound carries through the air vents. Mrs Goodman umm, she's one of those women who umm, like to be noisy when they're umm, y'know?"

"Ahh," Ray nodded, making hasty notes.

"Would this butler be an African American guy?" Angelo asked and the man nodded.

"Yeah. Gabe. I don't know the rest of his name, but he's a nice guy. When they are both out at work, he sometimes comes down here and shares a beer with me and a game of D and D."

"D and D?"

"Dungeons and Dragons."

"Oh," Angelo replied.

Ray grinned. "You don't know D and D?"

Angelo shook his head. "Never heard of it."

"My god, what do you do of an evening?"

"Well I don't play D and D."

"You need to educate your partner here," the man said to Ray, who laughed.

"Did the Goodmans fight much?" Angelo asked.

"No, I wouldn't say so at all. I've never heard them yell like they did earlier tonight. From what I heard, I guess he came home and found the two of them in flagrante delicto."

"It would seem that way," Angelo nodded.

"Is Gabe okay?"

"I'm afraid he's dead."

"What? Who killed him?"

"I'm afraid I can't elaborate on that at this time."

"That's a damn shame."

"So would you say that tonight's behaviour was odd or out of character?" Ray asked.

"Definitely. Just like so many others in this place lately. It must be a phase of the moon or something. Everyone is going a little nuts. It's kind of scary if I'm honest."

"If you think of anything else that might be relevant, call us huh?" Angelo said as he handed over his card.

"Sure."

The two detectives walked down the corridor towards number one twenty eight.

"Well that went okay," Ray said.

"Yeah, nice guy I guess."

"Next we have Clarissa and Deidre Pilcranton."

110

"Oh yeah." Angelo grinned as he remembered the elderly sisters. "Ready for some china tea and tales of Grandfather's epic foreign travels?"

Ray laughed aloud. "I guess so."

Deidre Pilcranton smiled with genuine warmth as she recognised the handsome police officer. "Well hello again, Officer, won't you both come in?"

"Thank you Ma'am," Angelo said and followed her inside.

"Clarry dear. It's the police officers again."

"We're sorry to bother you this late Miss Pilcranton," Ray said.

"Don't apologise. My sister and I may be getting on in years but we're neither deaf, nor stupid. We're not at all surprised to be entertaining you both again."

"We were called to an incident in the penthouse apartment, I'm afraid there's been another two deaths. Mr Goodman and the butler, Gabe."

"Oh," Clarissa said from behind, having entered the room. "Gabe is such a nice man. What a terrible shame. He always calls in a couple of times a week to make sure we're all right. How many young men nowadays would do that?"

"It's always the good ones that go first dear," Deidre said and Clarissa nodded.

"Did you hear anything from upstairs at all?" Ray asked. "Anything unusual or strange?"

The two sisters exchanged a quick glance and the two detectives guessed that yes, they had indeed heard something.

"Oh yes we did," Clarissa nodded. "Since earlier this evening we've been hearing what can only be one thing."

"And that would be?" Angelo asked.

"Well," Deidre hesitated. "How can I put it delicately?"

"Oh don't be so prim dear," Clarissa snapped. "Mrs Goodman was obviously fucking the butler."

Ray's mouth fell open at the sight, and sound, of this genteel old lady dropping the F bomb in such a matter of fact way. He noticed that Angelo's eyebrows had risen a good few inches in surprise and almost laughed aloud.

"Clarry, your language," Deidre whispered. The two sisters looked at each other in silence, and then burst out laughing.

"The language that's been filtering down here via the air vents was far worse, and well you know it, Sister." Clarissa said when they had both stopped laughing.

Deidre nodded. "Yes. We were given a running commentary on almost everything they were doing to each other, and they were at it since just before six this evening."

"It made me wonder whether we should hire a butler ourselves," Clarissa remarked, which sent both sisters into a fresh fit of giggles. Angelo and Ray grinned.

Forty minutes later, a pair of relieved detectives left the Pilcranton apartment and almost ran down the corridor.

"Jeez, did those old ladies almost rape us?" Angelo asked.

"It certainly seemed that way to me," Ray nodded. "One of them told me she wasn't wearing any underwear."

"Was that the one who kept stroking my thigh, or the other one?" Angelo asked.

"They didn't do anything like that the last time we interviewed them, did they?"

"No. They were two stiff old ladies as far as I remember. They made us drink china tea and regaled us with boring stories of their grandfather's foreign travels. No mention of their underwear, and I don't remember having my thigh handled."

"I guess we can assume that they're both turning Gainsford on us."

Angelo nodded. "Well it beats being shot at I guess. Okay, who do we have in one thirty one?"

"Tommy Chang," Ray replied. "The martial arts guy."

"The ninja guy? Oh shit, that's all we need."

"Ninja guy?"

"I christened him the ninja guy because of all the martial arts stuff. Don't you remember seeing all that stuff hanging on the walls in his place?"

"Yeah, the swords and, oh, shit."

"Right."

As they walked down the corridor and turned the corner, they passed apartment one thirty, and noticed the front door standing open.

"I thought the guy in this one was away," Angelo said.

"He is," Ray replied, reaching for his gun. "Jason Rackman. He's in Europe, working on setting up an outpost for the company he works for."

Angelo approached the open doorway, reaching for his own gun. "Mr Rackman?" he called. "Jason Rackman? This is the police. Mr Rackman? Mr

Rackman, we're coming in." With a nod to Ray, Angelo stepped inside the door, noticing a door immediately to his left, and another a little further ahead on the right. He motioned to Ray that he would take the left, and Ray nodded, moving ahead to the door on the right.

Angelo's door turned out to be a closet, so he turned and headed towards where Ray was reaching toward the handle of the door on the right. Before he could grasp the knob, the door flung open, catching him a glancing blow to the side of the head. Knocked off balance and shocked from the sudden blow, Ray stepped back into Angelo, dropped his gun, and the two of them stumbled and almost fell to the ground. A shriek filled the hallway, and both detectives saw the ninja guy standing over them, naked to the waist. The samurai sword in his hands reflected the overhead light, which glinted along the blade as he held it aloft and continued shrieking some foreign words that neither of them understood. Fumbling to get out from under Ray's body, Angelo struggled to raise his own gun, and by the time Ray had moved out of the way, the still shrieking man had disappeared out through the still open front door. They leapt to their feet and headed for the door, which slammed firmly shut in their faces, the bang echoing along the hallway. Despite using their combined body weight, and finally shooting off the locks, the door refused to open. When the light bulb exploded and sent them both tumbling into darkness, a fear stronger than either had experienced in a long time, embraced them.

PSYCHOMANTEUM

21

It waited beyond the portal, knowing that soon, It would not need to keep traversing back and forth. The time when It could remain in the world of the humans was close. The groundwork had been done. The residents of Gainsford House were producing plenty of delicious negative energy, and daily travel between the two dimensions would no longer be necessary. It would be able to dwell beyond the portal for an extended period. This also meant that the Portal Keeper would no longer be essential. It had become aware that having a human under control would provide something valuable, a mouthpiece. With a human through which to interact with the others on this side of the portal, It could be far more effective. If they were coerced into compliance, they would be easier to control. A human through which to talk, to provide a back-story, a legend, the others could become an army, a perpetual energy producing machine from which It could feed. As It grew and evolved, to become the apotheosis of its kind, the humans would have a new deity to worship and obey.

What was once Harlon, but which was now no more than a physical shell that resembled what he used to be, descended the stairs and walked across the lobby towards the concierge's desk. The young woman shuddered as she looked into the eyes of the man who approached her, a half smile frozen upon her lips. It looked like Harlon Drake, but something about his demeanour told her this was not Harlon Drake at all, and she registered the icy finger that traced its way down her spine. Using all of her mental strength, she tried to force her lips into a smile.

"Good evening, Mr Drake. Is everything okay?"

He looked back at her with an expression that she guessed must be an attempt at a smile. This was a smile that conveyed no affection, but a rictus, filled with foreboding from which she knew she should run. Her legs refused to move, and she remained rooted to the spot, the corners of her mouth twitching with the effort of forcing a smile at the terrifying apparition that stood before her.

"Everything is wonderful. More wonderful than I ever believed possible."

"Is there anything I can do for you?" she asked, her voice faltering more than once.

"Yes, there is indeed. You can follow me."

"Follow you? Where?"

"Up. We must gather the people together, and then everything can be wonderful for you all."

"Oh I can't leave my station. My job is to remain here at the desk."

"But you must follow." He stepped forward and leaned across the desk.

"I can't," she replied, on the verge of tears as she took a step back and winced as the filing cabinet dug into her back. She knew there was nowhere else to retreat and wanted to cry out in terror but her mouth and throat were frozen in fear.

"You must trust me, there will be no pain if you trust me, and follow." He came round the side of the desk and reached for her hand.

"Please, don't," she begged as his hand gripped hers and the icy chill worked its way up her arm.

"You will all be my soldiers, my army with which I shall conquer and vanquish the enemy that has taken over your world. Together we will cleanse the world of the rank stench of love for life that smothers it. We will rid it of the putrefying lust for living that squeezes the life from its lungs."

"Yes, I understand," she nodded as her mind cleared and the fear melted away. How clear everything was now, and how stupid she was to have been frightened, she thought to herself as she stepped forward.

22

Up on the twenty-second floor, Angelo and Ray cried out in shock as they were plunged into suffocating darkness.

"Shit," Ray yelled. "Angelo? Where are you? Talk to me huh."

"I'm here," Angelo gasped from his right, his hand flailing in front. "Take my hand."

"Where is it?" He flailed his arm in mid-air, grasping frantically when something bumped into his wrist. "What was that?"

"That's me. Bring your hand over this way again."

"Okay, I got you. Just breathe for a moment huh? Shit, I was always terrified of the dark as a kid."

"Stay together and stay calm," Angelo replied, as much for his own benefit as his partner's. "We need to get out of this apartment and back into the corridor. The front door is here somewhere; feel for it with your spare hand."

"Yeah, okay." Ray moved forward, pulling Angelo along as he slid his hand along the wall to his left. Now he had something positive to focus on, he was able to push the fear to the back of his mind and stay in cop mode.

"I got a wall this side," Angelo said as he reached out with his spare hand and touched the opposite wall of the hallway.

"Me too. Can you remember how far inside we came?"

"Umm, not too far. About ten or fifteen feet at a guess. There was a doorway on each side, mine was a closet."

"Mine was where the ninja guy came from. I have the doorframe now, the door is still open."

"Okay," Angelo nodded. "The closet door should be a little further up on my side then. I remember your door was further inside than mine. Just keep going forwards."

"We still have to get the door open y'know," Ray said. "We shot the locks off but it still wouldn't open, remember?"

"Don't worry. If I have to kick the door in with my bare feet, we're getting out of here."

"Yeah," Ray said, strengthened by the conviction in his partner's voice. "And we can always shoot a big enough hole in it to give us a head start if need be."

"Right, so there's no need to panic huh? Okay, I have the closet door here. The front door is a couple of steps more."

Suddenly, the hallway jumped into view as a blue light pierced the darkness.

Angelo jumped and cried out, startled almost out of his wits. "What the fuck?" he yelled.

"It's okay, it's my cell phone," Ray said. "Why didn't we think of it earlier? Come on, get yours out and use the light."

"Oh shit." Angelo closed his eyes and waited for his heart to calm. Fumbling in his pocket, he yanked open his phone and the light in the hallway strengthened. "Good thinking."

"There's one problem," Ray said.

"What?"

"You're still holding my hand."

Angelo let go of Ray's hand and was glad it was still too dark for his partner to see him blushing. "Yeah, sorry." A moment of silence was quickly followed by Ray's unmistakeable laughter, and despite the gravity of the situation, Angelo joined in.

"This has got to be the weirdest shit ever," Ray said and Angelo nodded.

"I won't argue with you on that one."

"How the fuck are we to explain this to the guys back at the precinct?"

"I haven't the faintest idea, but I'd be glad to be back there and finding out and not stuck in here in the dark with a crazy ninja guy hiding somewhere in the shadows."

"Shit, I forgot about him. He ran outside though, so we know he ain't in here with us."

"Yeah, that's one small mercy I guess. When we do get out though, remember he could be anywhere so be ready."

"And hope the lights haven't gone off everywhere in the building," Ray said.

"Oh shit, I hope not."

By the time Harlon reached the apartment of Doug Morrison on the fourth floor, he had accumulated a large band of willing followers, all gleaned from the still occupied apartments. So far, only two had refused to follow, and both of those were now dead. The group stood and swayed slightly as he knocked on the old man's door.

"What do you want?"

"Hey, Doug. It's me, Harlon Drake. Open the door, please." He heard the sound of the security chain being unhooked, and then a click as the old man released the catch. With a strength way beyond that of any normal human, Harlon shoved the door open and stepped inside. The old man fell back against the wall and raised his walking stick in a defensive gesture.

"What's the meaning of this?" he demanded, allowing his mind to take him back to the jungles of Vietnam. Young, strong, and defiant once again, Doug stood straight and looked Harlon in the eyes. "Get out of my home or I'll call the police."

"Fear not, Doug. We're here to help you, to take you to safety. Come with us."

"I may not be able to see you clearly, but I can sure as hell smell you and you smell wrong, Mr Drake. There ain't no way I'm following you smelling like that, so you can turn right around and get out of my home now."

"I cannot save you if you do not follow."

"Okay," Doug replied, thinking quickly. "I'm sorry for doubting you. Lead the way."

"You are wise, Doug," Harlon said, his eyes looking through the old man rather than at him. He turned and led the way out of the apartment and beckoned Doug to join the small crowd that stood at the door. Flinching from the icy fingers that tried to grip his arms, Doug raised his walking stick and brought it smartly down upon the head of the young female concierge who reached for him. As she fell, he leapt over her prone body and hurtled down the corridor as fast as his aged legs would carry him, his stick waving side to side to guide him in his flight. In his mind, he was back in the jungle and searching for cover in which to hide from the Viet Cong. Having lived in Gainsford House for many years, he knew exactly where he was going, and despite knowing that the next few seconds were going to be painful, he knew he had no choice. He had seen many things during his life, some terrible and unforgettable horrors, and he prided himself on knowing when something was badly off with a situation. Knowing that something was wrong here in the building, he knew he had to get out, and was willing to die trying. The jungle smells and sounds came back to him as he ran, the sounds of startled birds and crumpled undergrowth rang in his ears as he finally spied his quarry up ahead. With a cry of both fear and exalted triumph, the young soldier threw himself into the hole, the jungle swallowing him up immediately.

George, Gainsford House's maintenance man, picked up his toolbox and fumbled in his pocket for his keys. It had taken him over an hour to unblock the bath drain and repair the waste disposal in the kitchen, and with the owner on holiday, he had left the job as long as he could. Locking the door firmly behind him, he walked down the corridor toward the fifth floor elevator. The door to the stairs opened as he reached for the button to summon the elevator and out stepped Harlon Drake followed by a large crowd, many of whom he recognised. He was about to say hello when something made him hesitate, the greeting frozen on his lips. There was something odd about the way Mr Drake looked at him. Those eyes were a little too earnest, too intense, and he involuntarily shivered as he gazed back.

"Mr Drake," He nodded curtly at the crowd who stood silently behind him. His finger jabbed at the elevator button again, and he knew he was failing to avoid looking scared. Harlon said nothing, but continued gazing right into his eyes, before he suddenly lunged forward and grabbed George by the shoulders. The crowd followed as one, leaping at George and grabbing at him as he fought frantically to get away. At first, George fought the icy cold that made its way through his skin and into the core of his body, but when he felt his brain succumb and his thoughts become jumbled, he stopped fighting. In less than a minute, his mind opened suddenly wider than ever before, and he saw the world in a completely new way. His eyes widened as he embraced the new clarity, and knew how the world had gone wrong for all these years.

"Of course. We must cleanse the world, wash it clean."

Harlon nodded, and then led the way down the corridor.

Angelo reached for the door, his gun already in his hand, and pulled at what was left of the lever. The door opened easily and he frowned. Surprised, he glanced at Ray before yanking the door open and leaping out into the corridor, Ray hot on his heels. After checking the corridor in both directions, and finding it empty, they breathed a sigh of relief.

"You want to check for the ninja guy or get out and call for back up?" Ray asked.

"Do you really need to ask me that?"

120

"Just checking. Okay, which way is the elevator?"

"As far as I remember, the nearest one should be around the next corner."

"At least the lights are on out here," Ray said as they made their way up towards the right hand bend in the corridor."

"Yeah, but unless I'm losing it, they're darker than earlier."

"You're losing it," Ray grinned as they approached the corner and slowed.

After listening and hearing nothing for several seconds, they leapt from the cover of the wall and found the corridor ahead, empty of life. The elevator door stood halfway along, the light from its button almost matching those that hung from the ceiling. Running as quietly as they could, they made for the elevator and pressed the button. As they waited, the lights in the corridor dimmed further, and both detectives noticed.

"So I'm losing it am I?" Angelo asked.

"Whoa," Ray exclaimed. "Oh man this shit is too weird for me. I gotta get out."

"Hold it together a little while longer okay? You can lose it all you want when we're back in the doughnut shop down the block."

"Yeah, okay," Ray said after wiping his face with his hand. As the elevator door opened with a ping, the gaping maw beckoning to them, both hesitated.

"I umm, I'd rather take the stairs," Angelo said and Ray nodded.

"Me too." Together, they made for the door beside the elevator. With twenty-two floors to descend, they knew they would be tired but neither cared. "My legs are gonna suffer for this."

"Yeah, mine too," Angelo said, "but right now I couldn't give a shit. I just wanna get out of this shit hole and into New York's delicious fume filled air. I want traffic violations, hit and runs, stick ups and car jackings, not this spooky shit."

"I hear ya."

Their shoes echoed softly on the tiled steps as they continued their descent, and all was going well until they reached the fourteenth floor. Suddenly, a scream rang out from one of the apartments and both detectives stopped, rooted to the spot. Their training told them to go and investigate, but their survival instinct urged them to ignore it and run for their lives. Both struggled to make the right choice, and stood, mid stride as they fought with their fears.

Finally, Angelo swore and turned back. "Fuck it to hell." He cursed and made for the door into the corridor, Ray at his side instantly. With a nod, they burst through the door and stood back to back in the now silent corridor.

"Which direction did the scream come from?" Ray asked.

"It sounded close, maybe to our right."

"Yeah, it was definitely close, but it sounded dead ahead to me."

"Okay so we have two apartments in this bit of corridor," Angelo said. "So do we split up or stay together?"

"You're happy about meeting the ninja guy on your own?"

Angelo hesitated before replying. "Shit."

"Me neither. Okay, come on. Let's try down here first huh?"

The door to apartment eighty stood open, the interior dark and menacing. Using their cell phones, they found the hallway empty and reached in for the light switch. The light was dim but lit the place enough for them to see where they were going, and in less than a minute, they swept through the whole apartment and found it empty.

"Okay, let's try next door," Angelo said and Ray nodded.

Together, they crept along the corridor and stood in front of apartment seventy-nine. Ray reached out a hand and was about to try the door, when a cry split the air painfully. Leaping around in fright, both registered that a body was coming towards them fast. Something glinted in the rapidly dimming corridor lights and told them they had found the ninja guy, or more correctly, he had found them. After no more than a second's hesitation, both raised their guns and prepared to fire, when the door to apartment seventy-nine opened and a woman cried out.

"Come in, quickly," she screamed.

23

The young woman urged Angelo and Ray inside, her voice frantic. "Quickly," she urged when they hesitated, the shock of her sudden appearance rendering them temporarily unable to decide what to do. "Come on," she screamed at them, breaking the spell. The two detectives leapt inside and all three fell against the door. The yelling from outside ceased at once and the three heard nothing, despite pressing their ears against the door for several seconds before daring to breathe. As if driven by one mind, the two detectives knew they were once again inside one of the apartments, only this time a resident was with them. Both turned and raised their guns towards the frail looking woman who stood before them, wide eyed and breathing hard.

She raised both hands. "It's okay, I'm not like them," she indicated towards the front door with a nod of her head. "And so long as you remain inside here, you will be safe."

"What the fuck is going on?" Ray said, his voice quivering with obvious fear.

"Something awful is happening," she replied.

"No shit," Angelo replied.

"Everyone out there has gone nuts," Ray said, putting his gun away and running a hand through his hair.

"I know," she replied. "A terrible evil has taken up residence here, but inside this apartment we are safe."

"How come this place is so safe?" Angelo said as he too, put his gun away. "None of the other apartments have offered us much sanctuary."

"We are protected here, believe me. Come in and have some coffee. Are you hungry?" She picked up a candle and led the way into the kitchen, the many candles dotted around giving the place a romantic appeal.

"So we're back with the black curse from hell after all," Ray said and Angelo snorted.

"Huh?" the woman frowned.

"Something someone said the other day when I interviewed her. By the way, I'm Detective Stellman and this is Detective Lamora. I'm sorry, we should've introduced ourselves properly but the manner of our arrival kind of pushed it out of my mind."

"I know," she nodded. "Which one is Ray and which is Angelo?" The Detectives looked at each other, neither knowing how to react.

"What?" Ray said.

"Which is which?" she asked again. "I knew you were coming, I was told to wait for you and give you shelter. Listen, I know this is all going to sound crazy, but I beg you to listen and keep an open mind okay?"

"I'm Angelo, and we're listening."

"I'm Nessy Bellinger, and I'm a psychic."

"Oh fuck me," he said and turned away.

"Please listen," Nessy said in her most commanding voice. "You're Angelo Lamora. You're thirty-two and married to Theresa Garcia. You lost a baby eighteen months ago, a girl that you planned to name Anna Marie, after both your mothers. It was two months before she was due to be born and you still haven't gotten over the loss. Theresa wants another child but you're too scared to try, afraid of losing another one. Your mother was..."

"Enough," Angelo yelled, swallowing hard to avoid the hot tears that stung the back of his eyes. "How the fuck do you know all that?"

"My spirit guide Patty told me."

"That's crazy, you're crazy."

"How else could I know? Huh? Well how?"

"Psychics? Spirits? Come on for fuck's sake," he said as he angrily wiped away a tear from his cheek. It had been almost a week since he last thought of Anna Marie and apart from Ray, he had not told a soul. This woman could not have known about it unless Theresa herself had told her.

"Lady, I don't know what you're up to here," Ray said angrily, "but you're way outta line bringing that stuff up. Now either you tell us how you know, or I'm gonna arrest you myself."

"You never forgave your brother for taking Christy Merle away from you, did you?" Nessy said as she regarded Ray. "She was your first serious girlfriend and you were fifteen. You loved her so much that when he took her away from you so easily, you almost pushed him off the roof of the apartment block you lived in at the time. You used to go up there to play, and he was sitting near the edge and didn't see you come up behind him. When he left home a year later to join the Marines, you never spoke to him again, and haven't since."

"What the fuck?" Ray exclaimed, shooting a glance at Angelo.

"You never told me that," Angelo remarked and Ray blushed.

"It was a long time ago, kid's stuff." He had never told a living soul about this event, so he knew right away that the only way this woman could know about it, is if she had some kind of weird ESP. He believed right away, despite not wanting to, and knowing it seemed crazy.

"So what's going on here? What do you know?" he said as he took the coffee cup she offered him.

"Hey now, wait just a god damn minute here," Angelo said as he glared at Ray. "You mean to tell me you believe this shit? Just like that?"

"Yeah, just like that, and if you wanna survive, you will too."

"Holy shit I'm surrounded by crazies," Angelo said and headed for the door. Ray leapt up and grabbed him, spun him around and pinned him against the wall.

"Listen. I never told a single living soul about my brother and Christy Merle, nor how I almost pushed him off the roof. I was so ashamed of what I almost did that I never wanted to have to admit it to anyone. That's why I became a cop, to stop people who can't stop themselves doing what I almost did, and to pay back people like my brother who take from people and don't give a shit. The only way she could know about it is by having some kind of ESP or something, cos it isn't written down nowhere and I never told anyone who could've gossiped to her about it. Put aside your scepticism for a moment and listen. We've got nothing to lose by listening anyway, and it might just save our lives"

"Okay okay, loosen up for heaven's sake," Angelo said. Ray let him go and stepped back. "I'm listening."

"This all started about a week ago," Nessy said as they sat around the table and drank coffee. "Patty suddenly came to me and showed me what was to happen to Saul Benedict. That same night he was murdered. To cut a long story short, Patty says that this thing, whatever it is, is made of negative energy."

"Huh?" Angelo said.

"Okay, I'll try to explain simply. You know what energy is?"

Angelo nodded. "Yeah, electricity.

"Nuclear power," Ray added.

Nessy nodded. "Yes, both of those are examples of energy. We are energy too. Our brains make electricity. You ask your forensic people, they'll tell you it's true. You can measure it in a lab easily. Anyway, different forms of energy have different frequencies, different power levels."

Ray nodded. "I know about that. That's why my toaster blows up sometimes, a power surge or something the electrician said. The power is too high and the circuit can't take it."

"Right," Nessy nodded. "Everything that produces energy, produces energy of a different frequency, a different wavelength, a different power, call it what you want. Our brains have their own frequency too. Everyone's brain is a slightly different frequency, everyone is unique."

"Okay, so what has this got to do with what's going on here?" Angelo frowned.

"Our thoughts and emotions affect our brain's energy frequency. You know what happens when you stick your finger into a power socket?"

"You get fried," Ray said.

"Right," Nessy nodded, a nervous smile hovering on her lips. "So when you do something bad, like murder someone for instance, it affects your brain's energy frequency. The energy you give off at this changed frequency is the sort that will hurt you, just like sticking your finger into a power socket."

Angelo put his hands on his hips. "So if you do something nice, the energy your brain gives off won't hurt people? No socket fry ups?"

"No socket fry ups," Nessy declared. "This thing, whatever it is, is made of negative energy, and whenever someone does something bad, like murder for instance, it makes it stronger. It needs negative energy to get stronger, to grow, and it also gives off negative energy that affects people, as you've seen."

"So all the weird shit that's been going on is because this thing is affecting people?" Ray asked and she nodded.

"Yes. Some people are able to resist for longer than others, but sooner or later everyone will succumb."

"All this talk about negative energy and positive energy is confusing me," Ray.

Angelo nodded. "You don't say."

"Just think of it as the driving force behind your actions," Nessy explained. "If you want to do something good, if you are driven to do good, that is positive energy. If you're compelled to do something bad, that is negative energy."

"Like right and wrong," Ray said. "We're cops, we know all about right and wrong and how easy it is within a small community for wrong doing to perpetuate itself, run amok like an infection spreading among a population."

"That's right," Nessy nodded. "An infection. That's a good way to describe it. Doing bad things, evil things, makes this infection grow strong. Then it can spread to other people and make them do bad things too."

"And it's spread through this whole building," Angelo said.

"Yes. It took a week for it to consume everyone here, and it's affecting the actual building too, haven't you noticed?"

"We've been a little busy coping with the people and how they're affected by it," Ray said.

"Well the lights aren't working anymore," Nessy continued, "and I assume that nothing electrical will be working. Have you not noticed the smell out there?"

"No," Angelo shrugged. Ray shook his head.

"You will soon. The black stuff too."

"Black stuff," Ray asked. "What black stuff?"

"It's running down the corners of the walls like black sticky blood. It's like the building itself is rotting where it stands."

"And this thing is causing that too?" Angelo asked.

Nessy nodded. "Yes. The level of purely negative energy is affecting the fabric of the stonework. Energy affects physical things all the time. Ultrasound for instance. Your wife will have had a sonogram when she was pregnant." Angelo nodded. "The sound energy they use for that can pass right through your flesh. Radiation energy has a detrimental effect on the body. The sun's energy burns our skin. The energy given off by this thing has no problem adversely affecting the fabric of Gainsford House."

"What does it want?" Ray asked.

"To grow strong and spread everywhere I guess," Nessy said and shrugged. "It wants chaos, evil. It wants love, affection, and compassion to be gone. You see it cannot survive where those positive emotions are strong. The energy frequency of those emotions are dangerous for it, so it must make sure that no one feels them. It makes everyone do bad things all the time so they give off negative energy and feed it more."

"What is it? Where is it from?" Angelo asked.

"Patty said it doesn't have a name. She said we created it. Man created it, that it's a natural by-product of man's existence, but that it's got out of hand

127

now. Every time we think, every time we act on those thoughts, we are either strengthening or weakening it, and everyone on the planet is doing the same. She said it normally resides in another dimension of sorts, another kind of existence. There's something about this building or the ground it's built on that makes it easy for it to cross over here into our world. I don't fully understand, it all seemed way beyond me. Different dimensions and stuff like that? Now that does seem crazy."

"So if we created it," Angelo said. "If man created it by being what we are normally, then how the fuck do we kill it?"

"Can we kill it?" Ray asked.

"We can't kill it," Nessy replied.

"Now, wait a minute here," Angelo said as he rubbed his eyes. "I'm trying to get my head round this, so be patient with me okay. If we created this thing by thinking and acting as people do all the time, every single day, then surely we also created a good one."

"Huh?" Ray frowned.

"If we created this bad thing with our bad thoughts and evil actions, then I presume we also created a good thing out of our positive thoughts and good deeds. Am I going the right way or have I lost the plot?"

"Sounds obvious to me," Ray replied.

Nessy shrugged. "Umm, yeah. I suppose we did," she said without much conviction.

"Then why doesn't the good guy do battle with the bad guy?" Angelo continued.

Nessy closed her eyes and breathed slowly. For almost half a minute she stood, silent and still before opening her eyes and nodding. "Patty says that since we created it, willingly using our negative energies, we must also have an active hand in returning the balance of energies to a more positive charge. We created the negative energies that made it grow strong, so we must create the positive ones to bring balance back. We then destroy the portal."

"How do we create enough positive energy to put this shit right?" Ray asked. "Wanna hug or something?"

"You're doing it already," Nessy replied. "By knowing this is wrong, that this can't continue as it is, that it must be stopped, that is creating the right energies. The compassion for your world, for other people and the desire to preserve those things, that is how you do it."

Ray and Angelo exchanged another glance. "So we're doing it already?"

Nessy nodded. "Yes. That is why you are both here. That is also why this thing will not stop targeting you. It knows you can return it to subjugation and it will try its best to kill you. You can rest assured that everyone who has been adversely affected by this thing will try to kill you the moment they know you're around."

"Nice," Ray hissed.

"You said something about a portal. What's that?" Angelo asked.

"It's like a doorway. A way of getting from one place to another. It's the means by which the thing gets here, from its normal home."

"And what does this portal look like? Where is it?" Angelo asked.

"Well," Nessy blushed. "This is going to sound crazy."

"And the rest of it doesn't?" Ray exclaimed.

"When Patty shows me an image of the portal, it looks for all the world like a black framed mirror. She also says that this thing, whatever it is, needs a human to open this doorway."

"It needs a human?" Angelo exclaimed.

"One of us?" Ray said.

"Yeah."

"So how the fuck do we find out who that might be?" Angelo said.

"You ask me, and I'll tell you."

PSYCHOMANTEUM

24

By the time Harlon and his band of followers reached the twelfth floor, Its plan was becoming a reality. With enough of a push, these humans were so easily influenced into total chaos and It watched as each new willing act of cruelty added strength to its cause. When touched by a source whose existence depends upon negativity, evil, cruelty, and hate, they were so willing to drop their moral codes and let their wildest animal natures out. The human mind is a fragile thing, and It found the people easy to influence. It was as if chaos was their true nature, and the restrictions of morality imposed upon them as a society were no more than an affectation. Like a mask, they wear it to create an image of a restrained and genteel race. They maintain this mask of gentility and morality with great difficulty, yet fall into chaos and disorder so quickly and easily. How they welcome lawlessness with open arms, yet still fight to strengthen their society's self-imposed behavioural standards. How they struggle to uphold those standards whilst denying their true chaotic nature. How happy they must be, It thought, that they could now become as their true nature intended. They would deify It; worship It for helping them complete their evolution.

Harlon stopped walking and cocked his head slightly to the side, as if waiting for something. He raised both arms high into the air, spread his fingers wide, and allowed the dark energy to flow. It flowed through the Portal Keeper's veins, picking up traces of human energy along the way. These traces would make sure the other humans would accept this new controlling energy easily. Like a virus mimicking its host's cells, the dark energy would use the human energy traces to fool human minds into accepting it. Like starving famine victims, the crowd drank in this new darkness as if their lives depended upon it. Darkness coursed through their veins, a total disregard for life and an urge to create pain and suffering took over what was left of their minds. The corridor throbbed with evil, the fabric of the building pulsated with it, and as the crowd spread out in all directions, the darkness followed. Like ripples on a pond, It knew that as the people affected spread and affected more, the world of humans would soon be cleansed and pure again.

PSYCHOMANTEUM

George, the maintenance man, still carrying his toolbox, let himself into apartment sixty-eight, where he knew Jackson Grant lived with his wife Loretta and their new baby daughter Amy. Loretta, awoken by a sound from the nursery, yawned and climbed out of bed. Her husband Jackson was driven out of his dream by her screams and ran into the nursery. He was in time to see the maintenance man whom they had given coffee to a couple of days ago, plunge a screwdriver into her eye and through to the floorboards below. He ran back into the bedroom and over to the night stand where he took out the gun he kept there for protection. Shaking so hard he almost dropped the bullets, he fought to regain control of himself as he loaded the weapon and stood. The memory of seeing his wife die strengthened his resolve as he strode back to the nursery and emptied the gun into George's body. George dropped to the floor without a sound, and Jackson Grant ran to the cot, almost afraid to look inside. His scream rang throughout the twelfth floor and when he emerged from apartment sixty-eight, he was a changed man. In his left hand he held the screwdriver he took from where George had left it, embedded in Loretta's left eye. In his right, the newly reloaded gun. As he walked the corridor on the twelfth floor of Gainsford House, there was nothing of the old Jackson Grant left.

25

Nessy relaxed as she made sandwiches for the detectives. It had been a long time since she had visitors, and she enjoyed the company of these men. They weren't true believers, but they did not make fun of her like others often used to, especially when she was young. Another thing that was comforting, but odd, was that neither of them were followed by the usual throng of deceased relatives all eager to get a message across. Nessy noticed this new strangeness and frowned. Everyone has forebears, previous generations, and they all wish to pass on assurances of survival. The knife stopped in mid-air as Nessy listened to Patty assure her that these men did indeed have many loved ones who all wished to communicate their affections. She was happy and grateful when Patty told her that they had agreed to stand back until this business was over, so that Nessy would not be overwhelmed when she needed all her mental strength.

"Thank you," she said aloud.

"Huh? What for?" Angelo asked.

"Oh, sorry, I didn't mean you," she blushed. "Patty is here."

"Oh? What did she say?"

"I was wondering why I haven't been swamped by your relatives, and she was assuring me that all is well."

"Huh?" Angelo frowned.

"This ability I have. People often refer to it as a gift, and it is, for the most part. It does have its downsides though, and it can be a burden at times. Spirits know that I am aware of them, they can see my ability. I'm not sure how they know, but they do, and they tend to flock around me and beg me to pass messages to those still alive. It's the reason I'm something of a recluse. It can be overwhelming, they don't stop sometimes. Both of you two don't seem to have that ever present throng of spirits all shouting at me to tell you this or that, and I wondered why. Patty told me that your spirit families have agreed to hold back while this business is going on, so I can work without distraction."

"Oh," Angelo replied, not knowing what else to say.

"Work how?" Ray asked. "What does she mean work?"

"We have to do two things. First, we must drive the thing back through the portal to its own dimension. Then we destroy the portal so it cannot come back through."

"Sounds simple when you say it like that," Angelo said as he bit into the delicious sandwich.

Ray nodded. "Yeah. So why do I get the feeling that it's going to be anything but simple?"

"Does your friend Patty know if we're all going to make it through this?" Angelo said suddenly, looking Nessy right in the eyes.

"I guess she does but she isn't telling me, and I suppose I can't blame her. Would you tell someone if you knew they weren't going to make it through the night?"

"I guess not," Angelo shrugged.

"How are we to drive it back to its own dimension?" Ray asked.

"Patty hasn't gone into detail about that," Nessy admitted. "She says she will tell us when it's time to move, that we're to remain here until then and not leave this apartment for any reason whatsoever."

"So we gotta sit here while everyone outside goes nuts and murders each other, and the only two cops in the building do nothing about it?" Ray asked. "That goes against everything I stand for."

"Me too," Angelo nodded. "We can't sit here and do nothing. There's a crazy guy on the loose with a samurai sword, he almost killed us a few floors up and almost got us again right outside your front door. God only knows how many others he's killed since then. We have to get some back up over here at least. Are the phones working?"

"No," she replied, indicating her landline. Angelo picked up the receiver and listened to the silence. "My cell phone isn't working either."

"Neither are ours," Ray said.

"Patty said that everything electrical, everything that uses any form of energy, is being drained by the thing. That's why the lights went off and it's so cold, the light and heat are forms of energy and it's using them as fuel."

"We're going to have to get out and summon some help," Angelo said. "Did your friend Patty say how long we're to sit here and wait?"

"Not exactly, but she seemed to indicate that it would all be over by sunrise. She said the war would be either won or lost by sunrise."

"Okay well I suggest we," Ray began but the scream cut him off and everyone listened in stunned silence. The woman's scream was one of torment and agony, and both detectives' mouths fell open in shock.

"Oh fuck," Ray hissed as he reached for his gun.

"That's Janey Conway from the apartment directly below mine," Nessy said. "The sound carries through the air vents."

"What apartment is she in?" Angelo asked.

"Seventy four, but you can't leave here. Please stay. Trust Patty, she knows what she's doing."

"Listen," Ray said as he and Angelo walked towards the front door. "We have to go and investigate. We're cops, it's what we do. We'll come right back as soon as we've taken a look. She may be needing help down there."

"What's the quickest way to her apartment?" Angelo asked.

"Turn left out of here and the stairs are a few steps down the corridor, not far. When you get to the floor below, turn left and seventy-four is the first door you come to. Each floor is laid out exactly the same."

"Okay," Angelo nodded. "Don't open the door to anyone but us okay? We'll be back soon, I promise."

"Okay," Nessy nodded, a weak smile faltering on her lips as she opened the front door and watched them disappear. A tear escaped as she shut the door, knowing what was to come for the two detectives. She wished she could do something to ease the coming suffering but Patty had made her promise to wait inside, and she had no intention of disobeying. However strong her interest in the life after this one, however much she yearned to find out what kind of survival she can expect, she had no desire to find out just yet. Despite the burdens her gift heaped upon her, Nessy loved living and believed she had much still to achieve in life.

Angelo and Ray made their way as quietly as possible to the stairs and descended to the floor below. Halfway down, Ray stopped dead and peered over the railing.

"What?" Angelo hissed.

"Look."

Angelo leaned over the railing, the shock registering on his face as he watched the floors below disappear into a black void one by one. The darkness creeping up towards them like a slowly rising tide.

"What the fuck is that?"

135

"I've no idea, but I vote we hurry up before we have to find out."

"Agreed," Angelo nodded and plunged down the last few steps to the thirteenth floor. They listened at the door and hearing nothing, opened it gently and stepped through. Ray hissed and Angelo looked, to see him nodding towards a door ten feet to their left. He nodded back and together, they made their way to apartment seventy-four. The door was ajar, but not enough for them to see in, and Angelo readied himself.

"Hey Angelo, promise me something."

"What? Can't this wait?"

"No. Promise me that if something happens to me, you'll let my parents know I was a good guy."

"I promise. And you promise me you'll look out for Theresa if anything happens to me. She doesn't have any family left, so be a friend to her until my family arrive and take her in okay?"

"I promise."

"Okay, you ready?" Ray nodded and Angelo gently pushed the door open to reveal the hallway in total darkness. Ray's fingers scrabbled for the light switch, and both heard the click but no light came. Using their cell phones to light the way, they made their way quietly along the hall. The closet to the left held no surprises, and the door to the right opened to reveal a small bathroom with toilet and basin. Another door was ajar further down to the left, and the door directly ahead was closed. The corridor turned ninety degrees left and disappeared. The room to the left was a bedroom, the bed having been recently used and not remade. An untidy pile of clothes lay in a heap in a corner, and a door to an en suite bathroom stood open.

The turn in the corridor revealed a short hallway, at the end of which was another bedroom, this one unused and obviously a guest room. Its en suite was also empty of surprises, and the pair returned to the closed door at the end of the short hall. They knew from Nessy's apartment above, that this door led into the sitting room and beyond that, the kitchen.

"You ready?" Ray hissed as quietly as he could.

"Hell no," Angelo hissed back. "Are you?"

"Are you scared?"

"Terrified. You?"

"Scared shitless."

"Now we have that little psycho drama out of the way, can we go in the room now and deal with the bad guy?" Angelo said.

Ray almost burst out laughing but stopped himself in time. "Be my guest."

"Thanks. On three. One, two, three." They burst into the room and swung around, taking in the whole room in less than two seconds. The lights from their cell phones did not reach far, but the open curtains at the large windows let in plenty of bright moonlight and the room was fairly well lit. After making sure no one was hiding behind the large leather sofa, they turned towards the kitchen. Halfway across the room, the temperature dropped suddenly by several degrees and both stopped in their tracks. Angelo remembered seeing the tide of darkness coming up the stairwell, and the creeping feeling of horror it gave him.

"I guess the dark we saw coming up the stairs has reached this floor," he said.

"I guess so," Ray replied and swallowed hard. Angelo heard the sound and worried for his partner. He was as scared as Ray but was able to hide it better. He wished Ray were better at hiding it, for watching him slowly lose it was affecting him more than he wanted to admit. He did not want to have to deal with Ray if he panicked, especially as he was the better shot of the two of them. With a gun in his hand, Ray was deadly, and Angelo feared what might happen if his partner became adversely affected by whatever was going on. He wanted to suggest Ray give up his gun, but knew he would probably shoot him for even suggesting it. Better judgement told him to hold his tongue and hope he could help Ray hold himself together. Before he took another step forwards, they both heard the growl. From somewhere to Ray's left, the distinct growl emanated from the corner of the room, where a large bookcase and a huge pot plant met.

"Oh shit, a dog," Ray said and turned.

"Nessy didn't say anything about a dog," Angelo said.

"Remind me to notify her of that later on huh?"

"With pleasure. Can you see it?"

"Just a shape, nothing distinct. Whatever kind of dog it is, it's not that big."

"Thank heavens for that," Angelo replied. "The last thing we need is a crazed Rottweiler to deal with."

"Don't even joke about that," Ray admonished. "Not in this building, not tonight okay?"

"Sorry," Angelo grinned. "Are you okay dealing with the dog while I check out the kitchen?"

"Sure, but be careful okay?"

"You too."

Angelo crept forwards, the moonlight glinting off the kitchen surfaces and he was pleased to notice that the woman who lived here liked shiny cupboard doors. The shiny surfaces reflected the moonlight and allowed Angelo to get a good view of the entire kitchen. He leapt through the door and the smell hit him before he knew what he was looking at. He had initially thought that the woman had been interrupted whilst making a meal, for something was laid out on the counter top, but now he knew what it was and he exclaimed in shock.

"Oh Jesus Christ." He turned away, his hand going instinctively to his mouth.

"What's going on?" Ray's voice called, the concern obvious in his tone.

"She's dead," Angelo replied. "Very, dead."

"Anyone else around?"

"No. How's the dog?"

"Still growling from the shadows but it's too scared to do anything yet."

"Okay, you wanna head back upstairs or should we make our way down and try to get out?"

"How are you for ammo?" Ray asked.

"I have half a magazine and a full spare. You?"

"Same here."

"We have another twelve floors below this one, that's twenty four flights of stairs. We can avoid the corridors altogether and remain on the stairs and be out within ten minutes. No matter what we hear, we get down and get out."

"What if we meet someone on their way up?" Ray said.

"Then we deal with the situation as it arises."

"In the dark, with just our cell phones for light? There are no windows in the stairwell, so we won't enjoy the moonlight. What if we meet the ninja guy? What if we meet someone else with a crazed Rottweiler?"

"Hey, you said not to mention that," Angelo said.

"I said don't joke about it, not don't mention it. I'm being serious now."

"I wonder if there are any flashlights in this apartment," Angelo said.

"Hell yeah, and spare batteries too. Nessy said anything that runs on energy will be drained, so we'll need spares to make it all the way down."

"Okay, I'll take a look around," Angelo said. "You stay with the dog and I'll see what I can find."

"Right, and don't take too long huh? This place is creeping me out like you wouldn't believe."

"Like I wouldn't believe?" Angelo replied. "You wanna maybe place a wager on that my friend?" He heard Ray snicker. Two large flashlights stood on a shelf under the sink, together with a box of spare batteries. On the windowsill was a hurricane lamp, obviously decorative here but still functional. It was one of the type that needed a candle rather than liquid fuel, and some further rooting around gave up half a dozen short squat candles that Angelo reckoned would give a substantial light if the flashlights failed. The metallic tang of blood was clawing at his throat and he supposed it was soaking into his clothes too. Wanting nothing more than to get out of this building, he forced himself not to look at the woman's severed head that sat in the middle of the counter top, and made his way back towards the sitting room.

"Okay, I have two flashlights and a box of batteries, and a hurricane lamp with half a dozen candles."

"Good haul," Ray said, his eyes not leaving the corner from where the growl still emanated. "Let's go."

With Angelo guiding the way, Ray backed his way out of the room and shut the door on the dog. He lowered his gun and relaxed. Before he spoke, the sound of gunfire reached their ears.

"That's below us," Angelo said and Ray nodded.

"Well we can either sit it out here and give him or her time to go away, or go and investigate like good cops should."

"Let's give it a few minutes, and then carry on down the stairs," Angelo suggested.

"Okay. Five minutes and if we hear nothing, we go. Here, give me half those batteries and candles."

Five minutes later, Angelo peered out from the door of the apartment. Seeing no one around, he moved towards the door to the stairwell, Ray following close behind. Angelo put out his hand to push the door open and heard Ray curse.

"Shit. Maybe we shouldn't just leave the animal here on its own."

"What?" Angelo hissed in disbelief.

"It must be terrified. Maybe we should take it with us?"

"It's terrified with teeth," Angelo said. "Leave it alone. It can defend itself."

"Okay, you're probably right. It just seems a bit mean."

"It'll be fine," Angelo soothed. "A dog is not much use when you want to conquer the whole world now is it? If it's chaos this thing wants, then it needs people to create that chaos. Maybe we should go back up and get Nessy to come with us though."

"Would she agree to come?"

"Probably not. Okay, you ready? Let's do this." He pushed the door and put out his foot to step through. Before the foot touched the floor, the sound of gunfire rang out once again from somewhere below, then a couple of screams followed by running feet. Both men heard a door below opening, and the sounds of several people heading for the stairs. He put a finger to his lips and silently stepped towards the railing and peered over. Ray held the door open and watched the corridor.

26

Jackson Grant, gun in hand, strode along the corridor of floor twelve, a single thought held uppermost in his mind. His wife and daughter had been murdered and now everyone he met was going to pay. They would pay for all the years Loretta and Amy would no longer be able to live, and all the happiness he was not to share with them. There had been some weird stuff going on in Gainsford House this past week, and he had been okay with it so long as it left him and his family alone. Now it had blown his simple but happy life to shreds and Jackson's mind blew apart under the combined weight of weirdness and grief. Rounding a corner, he saw a small group of people coming towards him, several of whom he recognised immediately. With no more than a moment's hesitation, Jackson opened fire.

Two women and a man fell dead. Jackson recognised one of the women as the concierge from the lobby. The uniform badge told him who she was, the hole in her head preventing him from recognising her face. The other woman was vaguely familiar, an older woman whom he had seen in the elevator on a few occasions. The man was a stranger to Jackson, but he did not care. The rest of the crowd scattered, Jackson's gunfire rousing them into action. Bloody leg wounds did nothing to slow the panicked exodus as a large group of people escaped into the stairwell, one of whom now carried a massive wound to her right arm that bled profusely all over the floor. A man Jackson recognised from shared elevator rides approached him, arms outstretched. He mumbled strange sounds and stared into Jackson's eyes with a purposeful glare. Jackson raised his gun but an icy chill took hold of his fingers, crept along to his wrist and climbed up his arm. No matter how Jackson tried to fight it, he could not make his finger pull that trigger and as the man reached for him, Jackson knew he was suddenly terribly afraid.

Harlon reached for the man, clasping his head and pressing his fingertips into his temples. It, using Harlon's vocal chords to express itself verbally for the first time in hundreds of years, spat vehemence at the man.

"How dare you approach me with your fetid stinking lust for life, human? You and millions like you have infected this dimension with your poisonous niceness, your disgusting compassion and toxic need for love. How you delight in spreading your foulness everywhere you go with your upright morals and unwavering need to do good. You're everywhere, the world is ripe with your malodorous legacy, the air is thick with the taint of your horrible goodness. I mean to bring this dimension back to order, to stem the flow that has run rampant for far too long. From this moment you will regain your true nature as beasts of chaos, you will learn to embrace once again the invigorating thrill of fear that you mistakenly turned away from. You still long to free that part of yourselves that your adopted societal rules told you was undesirable, and how easily you open those prison doors. For so many centuries have your societies toiled to bring the order that you declare to be ideal, but how quickly you return to your natural state with so little encouragement from me. Embrace your true nature, human, embrace it."

Harlon dug his fingers into Jackson's temples as It shrieked, the energy coursing through him making his whole body vibrate. He heard the thrum in his ears and he thought back to when he was a kid and walked underneath electricity pylons and heard them sing. His body filled with such energy, as though he were some kind of crazy living dynamo, a powerhouse of unlimited energy. He felt like a god. The man in his grasp moaned, his eyes rolling up to leave the whites staring back, his lips pulled back in a grim rictus as his body went stiff. Harlon noticed a sudden and large erection make itself apparent from the man's groin, followed swiftly by the unmistakeable noise of his bowels being involuntarily voided, the smell confirming it seconds later. A sudden warmth caught Harlon's attention and he looked down in time to see the wet stain spread from Jackson's freshly emptied bladder spread to his own jeans. Jackson's body jerked as if in some kind of grand mal seizure and as the vomit ejected itself from his mouth, the head exploded under Harlon's grasp. Blood, bone and soft fleshy matter flew in all directions, spattering his face, the floor, and the walls for several feet around. Harlon let the body drop to the floor, and then headed towards the elevator. Despite power being drained from the building, It was able to ensure the elevator worked by channelling some of its own energy through Harlon's fingertips. With a ping, Harlon stepped out on the thirteenth floor, and worked his way around the apartments.

Angelo was so relieved to see the people head for the stairs that led down, that he almost burst into tears. Turning back to Ray, he tiptoed back to the door.

"There's quite a crowd down there. One of the guys is limping, so I guess he caught a bullet in the leg. Thankfully they're heading downstairs, so I vote we give them a minute or two before heading down." Ray nodded and was about to verbalise his agreement, when the ping of the nearby elevator caught their attention. Angelo grabbed him and hauled him through the stairwell door and both men ducked down under the small window. A few seconds of silence, then the sound of knocking on a door.

"That must be the apartment we just came from," Ray whispered.

"Sounds like it, yeah."

A minute later and the sound of frenzied barking made both men jump and Ray snickered. "Go get him boy."

Angelo's laugh froze on his lips as they both clearly heard the high-pitched yelp, followed by sickening silence.

"Oh shit," Ray said. "I knew we shouldn't have left the dog there."

"Dammit," Angelo hissed. "Fuck."

"Come on, let's get out of this crazy shit huh?"

"Hey I'm sorry man," Angelo said. "I insisted we leave the dog behind, and it's my fault he's now dead. I should've listened to you." He looked at Ray, hoping that this admittance of guilt would prevent his partner from holding it against him should the building succeed in influencing them both before they got out.

Ray slid a hand through his hair. "Neither of us can see into the future. Your reasons were valid, and I agreed at the time. At least it sounded as if it was quick for him, we can be grateful for that at least."

Angelo nodded. "Yeah, you're right. Come on, let's go."

Knowing that a few floors below was an unknown number of potential crazies, Angelo and Ray reluctantly decided it best not to use the flashlights they had stolen from Janey Conway's apartment. Gingerly feeling their way along in the total darkness, they crept down the stairs. At times, their fingers touched something wet and sticky, and they remembered Nessy telling them about the black ooze bleeding from the fabric of the building. Instinct told them to withdraw their hands in horror, but the fear of falling to the ground floor was greater than their disgust. One floor below, their cop's instinct got the better of them, and they decided to go and investigate the scene of the gunfire they had both heard. Slowly they opened the door to the main corridor, and after checking both ways with their flashlights and finding no one about, they stepped through.

Ray's foot sank into something mushy and he instinctively stepped back, bumping into Angelo. "Ew what the fuck is that?" He swung his flashlight down to the floor. "Oh shit," he gasped as he saw the headless body surrounded by a sea of bloody mush.

"Holy mother of Hades," Angelo hissed as he took in the gory scene. "What have we gotten into here, a horror movie set or something?"

"Where's his head?" Ray swung the flashlight around.

"I don't know but you can find this one. I got the last one."

"What last one?"

"Janey Conway," Angelo replied, nodding his head up toward the ceiling. "Sitting on the kitchen counter top and staring right at me. I'll be seeing her in my dreams for months, I just know it."

"Shit, I didn't know, you didn't say."

"I didn't want to worry you I guess."

"Why?" Ray demanded, standing straight up and glaring at his partner. "You thought I couldn't handle it or something?"

"Of course not," Angelo replied, worried suddenly at his partner's change of demeanour. "I didn't want you to have to find out. It's called caring, you heard of it lately? If you want to handle it, handle this one and leave me out of it. Go find the head yourself. In fact, why don't we check all of the apartments while we're here huh? You go that way and I'll go this way, and we'll meet round the other side with whomever we find. See ya later." Angelo strode down the corridor, worried for his friend and angry at the same time. He was calling his partner's bluff and prayed he would fall for it so he would not have to make the rounds of the apartments alone.

"Hey hey wait a minute," Ray called. "Wait up, man. I'm sorry okay? I guess this place and all this weird shit is getting to me."

Angelo stopped and silently sighed with relief before turning around and heading back to his partner's side. "I know. It's getting to me too. I have been thinking though, about what Nessy said."

"What?"

"About how to end this. She said we have to find the doorway that this thing is using and then destroy it."

"I thought we were getting out of here and calling for some backup," Ray said.

"I know, but do we want a truck load of cops in here who don't have a clue about what's going on, and all going nuts and shooting each other? Besides, what do we say when we call huh? Please come help us fight an invisible thing from another dimension who wants to bring the whole world to chaos. I'm too terrified to even think how Ted and the guys would receive that."

"I guess you have a point. They might just get in the way rather than help."

"We're the only ones who've been here from the start and seen how this has progressed. This is why we're able to believe this shit, because we've been through it from the get go. None of the other guys at the precinct would be able to accept any of this shit. I vote we give Nessy a chance before we call in the troops."

"Agreed," Ray nodded. "So you wanna go back up and talk to her?"

"I reckon we should. What about you? We must do what we both agree with, no splitting up or arguing or this place could turn either one of us or both into something neither of us wants to be."

"My instincts tell me to get the fuck out," Ray said, "but then if what Nessy says is true, then it will carry on. Maybe not in this building but in the next one along the street, or the one opposite. On any normal day, I would say you've gone crazy and report you to the boss as unfit for duty, but after what we've seen and experienced here, I have to reluctantly agree with you. We should give Nessy a chance. I for one don't want to be the one who refused to believe and brought about the end of the world."

"Me neither. Okay, let's go back up, and remember that whoever was in the elevator might be up there."

Ray nodded, and together they climbed silently back up the stairs.

Doug Morrison groaned in pain, but was pleased to feel the pain as it meant he was still alive. A stab of agony as he tried to pull himself up into a standing position told him he had probably broken his right wrist. Both of his elbows were sore but as his arm movement was not impeded to any great degree, he assumed they were not broken. His journey down the south side garbage chute had been terrifying but thankfully short, and had got him away from Harlon Drake, or whatever kind of evil possessed him. Doug had seen many things whilst serving his country, and had witnessed first-hand the sight of a voodoo zombie. He guessed that Gainsford House had become possessed by some bad voodoo spirits that were affecting the residents and causing them to become evil, and he wanted no part of it. He had always been a forthright and indomitable man and prided himself on his ability to act without hesitation when the shit hit the fan. Doug was not one to panic in times of crisis, but he was careful and not one for unnecessary risks, especially since his sight got so bad. He dragged some bags of garbage around himself to make a comfortable seat and settled down as best he could. He knew he was unable to climb out of the huge dumpster with a broken wrist, and he didn't want to shout for help with everyone going crazy around him. No, the best thing to do, he decided, was to wait it out. The tactic had served him well in Vietnam, and it would do the same now.

27

In apartment seventy-five, Cameron Walker and his husband Danny Velkiss returned from their honeymoon three days ago and found all sorts of weirdness going on at Gainsford House. They had enjoyed three wonderful weeks in the Seychelles and made friends with a British couple. Adam and Geoff were also honeymooning and the four were determined to remain friends despite the distance between them. Cameron and Danny were blissfully happy at having found the perfect woman to be surrogate for the child they waited to welcome into their lives. They were celebrating with an expensive Rioja when they heard the gunshots from below. By the time the second volley rang out, they were hiding in the bedroom closet, behind the secret panel they had installed that hid a small panic room. It would not keep anyone out once discovered; it relied on its camouflage for protection. From outside, it looked identical to all the other panels in the large walk in closet. The latching mechanism, hidden skilfully within the ceiling light fitting was a masterstroke, and one of which structural engineer Danny was especially proud. Inside was five feet by four, but big enough for them both to hide if necessary, and insulation on the walls helped cover any small noises they might make while hiding within. At one end was a small camping toilet and a wooden box containing half a dozen five-litre water bottles and several boxes of protein and energy bars. These most basic of facilities were to help make them comfortable in the event of an extended stay within the small cell.

Danny was most insistent that he build some kind of panic room for them both, but did not want to make its existence public knowledge. This is a risk one always takes when hiring a company to produce such an item, so they both agreed to do the job themselves. Cameron, being a highly qualified architect, designed the small space that Danny then built. The panel was so well camouflaged that it did not need to be solid, and the fact that no one other than themselves knew of its existence was their greatest ally. They practised getting into the small room many times, and decided to store a change of clothes and several changes of underwear inside, in case either of them was in the shower when the moment came. Spare cell phones, with their chargers were inside, as was a newly fitted electrical socket to supply any of their power needs. A laminated list of important telephone numbers was stuck to the wall, as was a copy of both men's wills, in the case of one or both of them not surviving. They clung to each other, scared for their safety for the first time in ages but determined that their love would see them through. That love would see them through anything, they reasoned, and continually reaffirmed it to each other.

Harlon stepped out of the elevator and looked both ways, tasting and smelling the air for humans. The sweet aroma of violent death came to him and he drank it in, the delicious scent leading him to apartment seventy-four. The door stood open, the smell of a sudden and fright-filled death still strong from within. Sniffing in the aroma, Harlon entered and followed his nose down the hallway to a closed door at the end. Flinging open the door, the residue of fear and desperation flowed over him like a tidal wave. It was beautiful and intoxicating and Harlon closed his eyes, wallowing in the fabulous experience. A release of pleasure from his groin caught Harlon's attention and he closed his eyes, thrilled at how vibrantly alive he felt for the first time in his life.

From out of nowhere, a stab of pain exploded in his left ankle and shot up his leg. The small white dog growled with as much menace as its reduced stature allowed, its jaws locked around his ankle. Reaching down, he wrenched it from his leg and hoisted it aloft, where it dangled and barked furiously at him. Wriggling its legs like a demented tentacled creature, the animal's fear reached Harlon and caused him to smile momentarily. Overriding its fear though, was an all-encompassing sense of protection that made Harlon sick to his stomach. The animal was imprinted upon its human owner and was compelled to protect them and their territory from all comers. Grabbing its two front legs, he tore the animal into two pieces, a last high-pitched squeal ending the onslaught.

The fear and pain of the animal's death revived Harlon from the nauseous quality its attachment and need to protect its owner had brought down upon him. He strode onwards relieved, the now familiar and delicious chill of fear and violence beckoning him forwards. As he entered the kitchen, he gasped aloud as the vestiges of Janey Conway's horrific death and dismemberment came to his energy. Caressing each body part reverently, Harlon made his way around the kitchen counters, soaking up the horror and fear like an addict on a pile of spilled heroine. Finally taking up her severed head, he clasped it, cheek to cheek to his own and ran his fingers through her blood soaked hair.

"Oh thank you my love," he whispered. "Such a wonderful gift you give me in opening yourself to the deepest depths of fear and horror. Your energy is not wasted, for you are now part of me forever. It was beautiful wasn't it, when you passed? Such purity can only be experienced through fear, horror and ultimate anguish and you my dear, you performed wonderfully. In embracing your true nature as you passed from this dimension, I can welcome you into mine. Here you will spend eternity in beautiful, honest, and undiluted chaos. You can allow your true nature to reign, unfettered by the false morality imposed by a cowardly society. This is my gift to you, as your true deity."

Putting down the severed head of Janey Conway, It, via Harlon, raised both arms upward, closed his eyes and exulted, a silent but energy filled cry of triumph. Dark energy spewed from his open mouth, the air throbbed with it and made the hairs on Janey Conway's dismembered arms, stand rigid. The tidal wave of darkness quickly spread beyond the confines of Janey Conway's kitchen and flowed throughout apartment seventy-four. It finally spilled out into the corridor and hurtled around the thirteenth floor. Into the fabric of the building Its dark energy flowed, the stone, concrete, metal and wood soaking it up like a sponge. Like a bolt of electricity the energy roared throughout Gainsford House, into every corner, every cobweb and crevice it raced. The air vents provided a perfect transport system and the energy waves coursed upward and down, through every floor, ceiling and wall. As It finally finished and Harlon closed his mouth, the remaining residents accepted the influence of this new darkness that washed over them invisibly from the fabric of their homes. Next door, in apartment seventy-five, in a secret compartment at the back of a large walk in closet, Danny crunched down hard and smiled as the wetness flowed over his tongue. A tough chewy bit was spat out with a frown, before he turned his attention to Cameron's other eye.

"Do you feel that?" Ray whispered as he and Angelo crouched behind the door that led from the stairwell, into the thirteenth floor corridor.

"What?"

"Close your eyes for a second."

"Close my eyes? What the fuck for?"

"Just do it will ya, for a second," Ray hissed, his eyes wide. Angelo shrugged and closed his eyes, then snapped them open again.

"Fuck, what is that?"

"See, I told you."

"It's like the building is breathing or something."

"Like a heartbeat maybe," Ray offered and Angelo nodded.

"Yeah. It's not a noise that I can hear, but I can feel it when I concentrate on it."

"Me too. Have you noticed the smell yet?"

"Yeah. It's almost familiar but I can't put a description on it. The black stuff is everywhere now too, running down the walls and dripping from the ceiling. It's dripped down the back of my neck a few times."

"Mine too. It's disgusting. I wonder what it is."

"I'd rather not know," Angelo replied. "It's thick and sticky to the touch."

"I wouldn't touch it if I were you," Ray said. "You never know what it might do to you."

Angelo ran a hand through his hair. "Shit, this is getting more like a bad horror movie with each minute that passes."

"Let's get back upstairs to Nessy."

"Maybe we should wait. We don't know where this guy is going, but he came up here from the floor below, so he could be going floor to floor. We don't want to run into him upstairs before we can get Nessy to open the door to us."

"But if he's going through each apartment, we have enough time," Ray said.

"How do we know he's going through each apartment? We can't assume anything."

"Well we can't follow him along the corridors, there's nowhere for us to hide. Besides, we'll hear the ping of the lift when he gets in down here, and that will give us enough time to get back into the stairwell upstairs and wait for him to pass through."

"Okay," Angelo nodded. "Let's do it."

Taking the stairs two at a time, Angelo and Ray raced up to the fourteenth floor and carefully peered through the small window in the door. What they saw of the corridor beyond was deserted, so they pressed their ears to the door and listened. Apart from the now regular throb that was felt rather than heard, silence greeted them. Angelo grabbed the doorknob and looked at Ray, who glanced quickly through the window once again, then nodded.

Thankful that the door did not creak, the two men leaned forwards, peered both ways down the corridor, and found it empty and silent. Ray took the initiative and walked to the left and the door to number eighty he knew was not far away, Angelo in hot pursuit on tiptoes. Ten feet from the door, they heard the ping from the elevator behind them. They turned on their heels and made to race back to the stairwell, when a voice from behind made them jump.

"Come on, quickly." Ray and Angelo turned, guns held out in front, to see Nessy peering from the open doorway to her apartment. "Hurry up," she urged and both men hurried inside.

"Perfect timing Ma'am," Angelo hissed as he leaned against the wall.

"Patty told me you were on your way back. You'll be safe now, come on and have some coffee to calm your nerves."

Over coffee, she asked them about Janey Conway and cried when Angelo told her she was dead. He left out a description of how she died, except to tell her that he thought it would have been quick.

"Thank you for trying to spare me the details," she replied as she wiped her eyes, "but I know you're lying."

"I guess you can't fool a psychic huh?" Ray said and she nodded.

"Something like that. Please tell me the truth."

"She was dismembered, in her kitchen. I'm sorry you lost a friend like that."

Nessy sobbed into the hand that had gone instinctively to her mouth as Angelo told her how Janey had died, and did not pull away when Ray put an arm around her shoulder.

"Do you know who did it?" she asked when she could speak.

"It could be any of the residents here," Ray said. "They seem to have all gone nuts, except for that guy Mitchell up top."

"Yeah he seemed normal," Angelo frowned. "It's weird how some folks aren't turning like all the others. Us two for instance. I know I'm being affected because my head is clearing now I'm in here and out of that horrible energy, but neither of us seems to be losing control completely."

"Some people are naturally stronger," Nessy explained. "Most people are followers, like sheep or bees. They cannot think for themselves and are easily influenced by someone with a more assertive energy. Now and then, you meet someone with a stronger personal energy and sense of personal sovereignty, which helps them resist for longer. Remain out there too long though, and you'll succumb just like the rest."

"Who is the guy that's doing all this?" Ray asked. "You said this thing needs a human through which to work. Who is it?"

"Harlon Drake."

"I might have known," Angelo said.

"I knew he was odd," Ray said. "He's the creepiest dude I've met in years; I knew there was something not right with him."

"We should've known when Nessy said the thing needs a human to work with," Angelo said and Ray nodded. "I've met all sorts of crazies during my time but he's the craziest of them all. No one has ever made me feel the way he did after that last interview. I was afraid and I'm man enough to admit it."

"Same here," Ray said.

"He's walking right past my door now," Nessy said. Angelo and Ray leapt up, guns in their hands and headed for the hallway. "It's okay; he doesn't know we're here. Patty is shielding us from his sight for now, we're safe in here." Both men relaxed and holstered their guns.

"So what do we have to do, kill the guy?" Angelo asked.

"We must lure him back to this portal. Once he realises that the portal is in danger, he will return to it. Patty says she will make sure the thing goes back to wherever it came from, and then we must destroy the portal so it can't come back."

"And then we kill Harlon Drake?" Ray said.

"Patty said there will be no need. She said that once it's returned to its own proper environment, it will stop its control of Mr Drake. She says there will be no need to kill him, and she said that if you do, the thing will just get another human to use anyway."

"At least we know who it's using, so we know who we're dealing with," Angelo said.

Ray nodded. "I guess it was probably him who killed the black guy on the twelfth floor too."

"Jackson Grant," Nessy said and closed her eyes. "A nice man with a lovely wife and beautiful baby daughter. How did he die?"

"Please don't ask," Angelo said and closed his eyes at the memory. The mess on the walls and floor told them that his missing head was not missing at all, it was everywhere. The lumps of unidentifiable mush they saw sticking to the walls, ceiling, and floor, and the spatters of blood that accompanied them told him what had happened. The slivers of bone embedded into the walls, all of these told him that whoever this man had been, his head had exploded, or been blown apart by something.

"We don't know, to tell the complete truth," Ray said, seeing his partner's distress. "We only know that he was a black guy because we saw his hands that still held onto his revolver. His head was missing." He chose not to tell her that it seemed as if his head had been blown up, but whatever had blown it up had not destroyed the rest of the body. Apart from having pissed himself and shit himself, judging from the smell, the rest of the body was intact.

"I wonder if his wife and daughter are okay," Nessy said quietly.

"I doubt they will have survived," Angelo said before she asked them to go and investigate, then immediately felt guilty. "We'll take a look later, when we've had a rest up and given Mr Drake time to get further away."

"No," Nessy said suddenly. "They are both dead and we cannot help them now. Patty is here and telling me that we will soon have to venture out to finish this. She asks that we try to relax and save our mental strength."

"Does anyone know where this portal thing is?" Ray asked.

"It's in Harlon Drake's apartment. He is responsible for opening the portal and allowing this thing through into our world, but he didn't do it knowingly. He is as much of an innocent victim as everyone here is. Patty wants us to be clear on this point, she is most insistent. She wants us to know that he was in no way an evil person who wanted to cause trouble just for thrills. He was duped by this thing, used by it, is still being used and she says that he will always suffer because of what has happened here."

"I understand," Angelo nodded and Nessy knew he was being truthful.

PSYCHOMANTEUM

28

It was strong, much stronger than the previous journey to this dimension. That last time, the previous Portal Keeper was strong enough to draw away from his duty and prevent what was now inevitable. This human dimension should never have been allowed to run out of control for so long; this should have been stopped the last time. The passage of so much extra time had seen the poison spewed by these humans almost stifle the whole dimension out of existence. It must not fail this time or this dimension would be lost forever. It knew that its own strength was sufficient to make the Portal Keeper redundant now, but still It kept Harlon locked away inside his own mind. He was safely under the impression that the ancestor he was so obsessed by was directing him towards some new and fabulous spiritual experience. This dimension was now at a critical stage, and It intended to succeed. Keeping the Portal Keeper on side in case he should be needed was good tactics.

It sensed the building housing the portal was now safely under its influence, the humans within quickly embracing the negative energies like starving children hungry for bread. It would soon be time to extend its area of influence to the neighbouring buildings, and in so doing, sweep the land clean of the human poison. Down at street level, an elderly man walking his dog stopped outside the entrance to Gainsford House, his eyes staring into space as his mind shut down under the weight of, something. One by one, as time ticked by, people passed just too close to Gainsford House and, like flies caught in the deadly spider's web, they wandered into the trap unaware of what lay ahead for them. Without warning, a woman opened her purse and took out the knife she always carried for protection. Walking to the man standing a few feet away who stared into space as he drank in the dark energy, she reached up and slit his throat. A scream pierced the night from across the street as It, refreshed by this new source of negative energy, used it to extend its trap a little further. Everyone who trod beyond the boundary into the deadly trap became a living energy factory for this cruel new master, the negative energy flowing out from them as they fought, injured and killed each other, making It stronger still.

PSYCHOMANTEUM

Gainsford House throbbed with negative energy; the fabric of the building itself was alive with it. The cells and molecules of the building changed under this new influence, and by the time Harlon made his way along the fifteenth floor corridor checking for anyone who might still resist, his feet squelched through the horrible smelling black liquid that now ran from the walls and puddled onto the floors. It was as if the building itself were rotting like flesh, the veins and arteries once vibrant with life now decomposing, becoming something disgusting and foul. It was comfortable and at home for the first time since venturing forth into this dimension, and knew that before too long, the mission would succeed. With enough violence, hate, and chaos, the human dimension would be under control again.

29

Angelo was dozing on Nessy Bellinger's couch when Ray gently shook him awake.

"Angelo, wake up. It's time to get going."

"Huh? What?"

"Have some coffee." Ray handed over the steaming cup and sat down. "Nessy says this spirit friend of hers says it's time to end this. We have time for a coffee and a pee, and then we have to go."

"Oh, okay." Angelo sat up and yawned. "What's the time?"

"Two thirty four in the morning."

"So we go to Harlon Drake's apartment, find this black framed mirror, and destroy it? Piece of cake."

"Wanna wager something on how far from simple this is gonna turn out to be?"

Angelo snorted in response. "Where's Nessy?"

"In the kitchen, washing dishes."

"Washing dishes? The world is coming to an end and the only person who knows anything about how to end this is doing dishes?"

"It helps me to relax," Nessy replied.

Angelo blushed. "Sorry, I didn't see you come in."

"That's okay. Something repetitive and mindless helps my mind stay calm when the spirit world is pushing in on me. It helps ground me, and believe me, we need to be grounded for this."

"It shouldn't take long in theory," Ray said. "Drake lives on floor twelve, which is two floors down, apartment seventy."

"Which is a few yards left of the stairs," Angelo said. "It's the first apartment we will come to if we turn left when exiting the stairwell."

"We find the mirror, which shouldn't take more than a minute or two, shoot it to smithereens and bingo, happy hour." Ray smiled, holding out his hands to the sides to emphasise the point. Angelo nodded and both men looked at Nessy for confirmation.

"And from the moment we leave the safety of this apartment," she said, "Patty will not be able to hide our intentions from it, whatever this thing is. It will know what we intend to do and will undoubtedly try to stop us, to protect itself and it's only means of traversing between its own dimension and ours."

"Shit," Angelo said as he screwed his eyes shut and ran a hand through his hair.

Ray paced the room and thumped the wall in frustration. "That means every person still alive out there will be after our blood. And we're gonna have to fight our way down there. How are you for ammo?"

"I have half a magazine and a spare, just like the last time you asked me."

"Sorry, I'm trying to keep a handle on this."

"We could find ourselves fighting women, kids even. Can you shoot a kid, Ray?"

"If that kid is trying to axe me through the skull, yeah. You?"

"Any ordinary day I'd say hell no, but I guess you never know what you're capable of until your life is in real danger. When you're pushed further than you ever thought it possible to be pushed, you'll do anything to satisfy that instinct to live I suppose."

"Remember though," Nessy said, "that every life you take and every aggressive act you do, brings you closer to the thing, and makes it a little easier for it to reach you."

"You mean we gotta do this without harming anyone?" Ray asked, his eyebrows raised in astonishment.

"As much as possible, yes."

"But that's impossible," Angelo replied.

"We must remain under the influence of the purest, most positive energy we can."

"How do we do that?" Ray asked.

"By focussing on that which brings forth the highest frequency of emotions."

"You're losing me," Angelo frowned and Ray nodded.

"Me too, sorry. Can you explain it for us in idiot proof terms?"

"Okay. This thing, whatever it is, needs badness, evil, chaos, right?" Angelo and Ray nodded. "It can't survive anywhere that this sort of energy doesn't rule supreme. Still with me?" Both men nodded again. "Anything other than pure darkness, evil and chaos, is anathema to it and downright deadly, according to Patty. So, we need to keep those opposite energies strong in our hearts and minds while we're outside of this apartment."

Ray grinned. "I get it. We gotta love them while they kill us."

"You're kidding, right?" Angelo said and glared at Nessy. "That's what we have to protect us, some flaky, new age, flower power, love thy neighbour shit? Tell me you're tugging our chains honey."

"Just listen please," Nessy begged. "What do you love more than anything else in the world?"

"My wife," Angelo replied without hesitation.

"Christy Merle," Ray whispered and blushed. Angelo saw his eyes welling up, and put a hand on his shoulder.

Nessy nodded. "There, that's what Patty means," she said as she pointed to Angelo's hand on Ray's shoulder. "That unconditional love for a fellow human is what she means, the all-consuming love we have for someone special, a spouse or child, parent perhaps; that will protect us better than your guns."

"It'll be hard to keep our hearts and minds on unconditional love when twenty people are trying to murder us," Ray said.

Angelo nodded. "How does Patty suggest we overcome that?"

"By keeping that emotion in the forefront of your minds," Nessy replied. "Even keeping the memory of it will help. By remembering that those crazies out there are people just like us. They're husbands, wives, sons, daughters, who just days ago, loved like you love your special people. They were Christy Merle's to someone not long ago."

"I guess being a cop for so long does tend to make you forget that those we deal with are people just like us," Angelo said. "It helps us cope with how awful it all is."

"If we didn't think of all the murderers and crazies as a different species to us," Ray said, "it would be much harder to do the job we do and remain objective. Of course we know that even murderers are husbands, fathers, mothers, and people's kids, but it helps us if we gloss over that fact when things are especially horrific."

"It helps us sleep at night and be able to look our families in the eye," Angelo shrugged.

Nessy nodded. "I understand that, but it's time to put that coping strategy aside now, for the next little while okay?" She looked from Angelo, to Ray, and both men nodded silently. "There's another thing we must be aware of while we're out there too. While outside this apartment, the thing will be trying to win you over, to influence you over to its own plan, whatever that might be. The moment you let your guard down and allow any negative thoughts into your mind, you'll be letting it into your head. Once it has a foothold in there, you're doomed."

"Okay," Ray said, rolling his head around. "Peace and love man," he said to Angelo, placing a hand over his heart and giving a slight blow. "You wanna hug?"

"Peace and love buddy," Angelo laughed, giving his partner a hug.

"It's time to go," Nessy said quietly. "May all that is good be with us."

"Amen, sister," Ray replied.

"Let's hope so," Angelo said.

"Hey do you know any songs from the sixties?" Ray asked as they made their way from the living room, along the hallway to the front door."

"No why?" Angelo frowned.

"Because they were into all that peace and love thing back then. They were experts on it. They must've had songs about peace and love and I thought if we sang one, it might help focus our minds or something."

"My aunt was a bit of a hippy," Angelo said. "According to my father anyway. He used to describe her as 'a bit funny' whenever I asked about her. Once I grew up, I realised he probably meant she smoked dope and had sex before marriage."

"Oh my god," Ray replied. "Perish the thought."

"He was kinda straight."

"You're telling me."

"Oh lord," Nessy said and both men looked at her.

"What's up?" Angelo said.

"Look through the spyhole," she said as she stepped aside. "See for yourself."

Angelo shut one eye and peered through the hole, to find himself staring at the profile of a man of about twenty-five. A grin turned his mouth up at one corner, and every few seconds he closed his eyes as his tongue swept across his lips. His attention was fixed on something to the left of the door, and whatever it was obviously excited him, as he was masturbating furiously. Craning his head to the side, Angelo studied the shadows that played on the corridor wall, and saw a prone figure, with another astride its abdomen. Using both arms to wield the huge carving knife, it chopped into the chest of the prone figure, its arms raising up between strikes. Angelo spun around.

"Shit. We're in trouble people."

"What?" Ray asked and Angelo stepped aside.

"Take a look for yourself," he said as he wiped a hand across his brow. As Ray looked through the spyhole, Angelo paced the hallway chanting 'peace and love' aloud. He heard it but he did not feel it.

"Holy crap," Ray said as he turned his back and leaned against the door.

"Remember, no negativity," Nessy said. She looked first at Angelo, then Ray and when both had nodded in reply, she took a deep breath and yanked the door open.

They young man grunted as his orgasm shook him, and turned to see Nessy and the two police officers exit from an apartment he had not even known existed. The last jets of semen splattered onto her skirt and his grin faltered slightly as they locked eyes.

"Don't look them in the eyes," Nessy crooned, her voice almost a lullaby and Angelo tried to respond in kind.

"Okay," he sang as he followed her towards the door to the stairwell.

"Peace and love," Ray sang from behind, his voice quiet but surprisingly melodious as Angelo listened. He never knew his partner had a good singing voice, and promised himself that he would get to know Ray on a more personal level once this craziness was done. As the stairwell door came into view, Angelo was aware of strong hands gripping his right shoulder and a loud grunt that filled the corridor. Trying hard not to fight back, he allowed himself to be yanked round through ninety degrees, to find himself eyeball to eyeball with Mr Mitchell, the dungeons and dragons player from the twenty-second floor. His hands and arms were red with the blood from the body that had been beneath him seconds before, and Angelo forced himself not to look. He closed his eyes, filled his mind with images of Theresa, and let his heart swell with love for her. Within seconds, the painful grip that held him firm disappeared and he opened his eyes to see Mr Mitchell wandering in the opposite direction up the corridor. He sighed aloud with relief and looked at Ray, to find him staring down at the body on the floor. Forcing his eyes away from the sight, he grabbed Ray's arm and gently pulled him around, crooning to him all the way.

"Hey buddy, peace and love remember? Remember how much you love everyone? Remember how you love Christy Merle? C'mon, let's go spread some love huh?"

Ray took a step towards them, then Angelo noticed something in his eyes change and he almost cried for his friend. He knew, in that moment, that his partner was lost to them and he could not prevent a tear from falling from the corner of one eye before he checked himself.

"She was fifteen," Ray hissed. "I interviewed her parents the other day and they introduced me to her. Look at her now; she was just a kid Angelo, a kid. I can't walk passed that, I can't. I have to get that asshole for what he did to her, I have to."

A tear trickled down Angelo's cheek as he gazed at Ray. "No. Please no. Stay with me. We're so close to finishing this. We can get him afterwards. She's out of pain now. Don't leave me, not now."

Ray looked at Angelo, the warmth in his eyes cooling until they were the colour of cold steel. "I can't. You go on, I'll catch up. I have to do this, I have to. Please understand."

Angelo said nothing; he nodded and let his hands drop from his partner's shoulders.

"We have to finish this," Nessy said, the urgency in her voice clear to them both.

"I'll be fine," Ray said. "Once I have this one asshole cuffed, I'll re-join you in apartment seventy."

"Keep Christy Merle in your mind okay buddy?" Angelo said and Ray nodded. With a wink, he turned and ran down the corridor.

"Come on," Nessy urged.

"He is my friend," Angelo hissed. "I should go with him."

"The best way to help him is to end this, and then he can be free. If we end this quickly, he won't be lost to you. If he succumbs to the influence of the thing, there's no telling how far away his mind will go, nor if he will ever recover once we do finish this."

Angelo hesitated, looking from Nessy, to the corridor, and back again, uncertain as to what he should do for the best. With a curse, he took hold of Nessy's shoulder and yanked her around. "Come on, let's do this, quickly."

Their journey to the stairwell was uninterrupted but as soon as they stood looking over the railing into the dark yawning chasm beneath, Angelo knew he had lost his peaceful state of mind. His flashlight did not penetrate far into the darkness, and both were aware of how tangible that darkness was as they crept their way down the steps. It was like icy fingers caressing their cheeks, holding their hands and whispering into their ears, and Angelo shuddered.

"Why is the floor wet?" he asked aloud, shining his flashlight at his feet and noticing the thick wet slime. "What is that?" He followed the trail of wet slime up the walls and saw where it had trickled down from somewhere beyond the reach of his flashlight. "It smells disgusting and it's been dripping from the ceiling and running down the walls for hours."

"It's a physical manifestation of negative energy."

"Huh?"

"Well, you see, it's," Nessy began but Angelo shushed her as the unmistakeable sounds of several people climbing the stairs reached their ears. As realisation hit home, both glared at each other with mouths open and eyes wide in terror.

"Someone's coming up," Angelo whispered as he switched off his flashlight.

"Sounds like they're a few floors down," she replied. "We could make twelve before they do if we hurry."

"We must hurry in silence," Angelo said and she nodded. Taking hold of her hand, he hurried her down the stairs quietly, hugging the walls in the asphyxiating blackness. Passing the door into the thirteenth floor corridor, Angelo was relieved that there was only one more floor to go, when he heard a sound that made his heart stop with fright. The man's cry was swiftly followed by several more and within seconds the baying crowd was racing up towards them.

"Quickly," he hissed and made for the stairs. "They know we're here." Reaching the half landing between the first and second flights that separated each floor, he stopped dead and urged Nessy to get behind him. He reached for his gun and waited for the footsteps to get closer. There was no way he was going to fill his heart with peace and love at this point, so he changed the half full magazine for the full one, and readied his gun. Wanting with all his heart to switch on his flashlight, Angelo fought the urge, knowing safety lay in the darkness. If he could not see, neither would the bunch of banshees that raced towards them, and he took comfort from the warm curves of Nessy's body that shivered in fright behind him.

It was all over in less than thirty seconds and it had taken a whole magazine to dispatch the eight bodies his flashlight exposed, and the couple he knew had fallen over the railing to their deaths twelve and a half floors below. With practiced ease, he changed the magazine for the half-full one, and hoped he would have enough to get them to Harlon Drake's apartment.

"Come on," he said to Nessy, who shivered beside him. "Not far now."

30

Ray raced along the corridor away from Angelo and Nessy, trying to stem the rising tide of fear that grew within his breast. Mr Mitchell was some way ahead; he heard his thudding footsteps in the distance. Rounding a ninety-degree turn, he shone his flashlight ahead in time to see Mitchell disappearing into one of the apartments. In his mind, Mitchell was no longer the man from the twenty-second floor who loved to play dungeons and dragons. Within Ray's troubled mind, he was his estranged older brother Chris, who stole the only woman he ever loved, just because he could. Ray knew he had to do this, for his own self respect. After all the years since he stood behind him on that rooftop and prepared to push him off, not once had he challenged him about stealing Christy Merle from him. He cried alone, hiding under the bed covers in the middle of the night and many times contemplated running away. Seeing Chris's face every day was a constant reminder of the pain, of his loss, and his own inadequacy.

The day Chris left home to join the marines was the first happy day Ray experienced in the four years since the rooftop incident, and from that day onwards, he never set eyes on his brother again. His parents questioned him about his repeated refusal to attend family events when Chris was in attendance, but Ray never told anyone the real reason why he would not acknowledge his existence. Chris wrote a couple of letters asking Ray what was wrong, but they went unanswered and after half a dozen phone calls were also ignored, he gave up trying and left Ray alone with his anger and grief.

Over the years, Ray's anger towards Chris changed and evolved. As he grew older, he realised with considerable anguish that his brother could only take Christy Merle from him if she wished to be taken away. The sudden understanding that she was complicit in the event was both painful and life changing. Women became objects to Ray. They were there only to satisfy his needs, he used them as and when he wished, after which he forgot them and moved on. He owed them no love, respect or honour, and there was no remorse as he threw them out at two in the morning in the pouring rain without so much as a cab fare home. Ray only had true compassion for women until they reached the age of sixteen, the age at which Christy Merle had allowed his brother to take her away from him.

To Ray, girl children were a different species to grown women, and the former were not related to the latter in his mind. Having no sisters with whom to have a healthy relationship, his troubled heart and angry mind survived only by dividing girls from women. He was loving and kind to girl children, as any good man should be. Once they passed sixteen though, they ceased to exist in his eyes. He loved kids, was trustworthy and honourable with them, and wanted a son of his own one day. The only problem was that Ray knew this would entail a relationship with a woman, the source of his disdain. He also knew there was no way to ensure a son would be the result of such a relationship. Ray knew that if he had a daughter, there would be problems when she reached sixteen. A child of his own, even a girl child, would be loved beyond measure. Ray was aware enough to know that if his feelings for her were to change, it would be too painful for him to bear. He thought back to the early days of his childhood love for Christy Merle as hot tears pricked at his eyes. He still loved her, but what he loved was the child Christy Merle had been, not the woman she became who betrayed him.

The front door to apartment eighty-one stood ajar and Ray approached with caution. Holding his gun with both hands, flashlight balanced along the barrel, he kicked the door open and swung the light from side to side. Seeing no one within, he entered and shut the door behind him. The layout was already familiar; every apartment in Gainsford House was laid out in exactly the same way, apart from the penthouse. The closet door to the left was closed and held no nasty surprises. He knew the door to his right led into a small bathroom, and remembered his shock at being attacked by the ninja guy on the twenty-second floor. That seemed like days ago, he thought as he approached the door and pressed his ear to the wood. For several seconds he listened but heard nothing, so yanked open the door and went in. Moments later, he shut the door behind him and approached the second door on the left, which he remembered as being a bedroom and en suite bathroom. Like the others so far, it was empty.

Only two more doors remained, and Ray approached the turn in the hallway. The one he saw in front of him led to the sitting room and kitchen beyond, whilst the one he knew lay at the end of the hall around the ninety-degree turn, was another bedroom with en suite bath. Leaping around from the safety of the turn in the hallway, Ray saw the door to the farthest bedroom standing wide open. Throwing caution to the wind, he ran up the short hallway and kicked the door so it banged against the wall within. His flashlight revealed an untidy but empty room, the bed rumpled and unmade. The en suite bath was empty but smelled strongly of the black oozing liquid that his flashlight revealed puddled in the bottom of the shower cubicle. Running back along the short hall, he glanced his flashlight back towards the front door in case anyone was waiting to catch him unawares, and stood before the door to the sitting room.

Mr Mitchell stood staring out the middle of the three large windows at the city that never sleeps. Neon signs flashed, car horns blared, and sirens wailed in the distance. Out there was normality, Ray thought, and he wished with all his heart that he could be there and leave all this crazy horror behind. He wanted to be sitting at his desk back at the precinct, laughing with Angelo. He wanted to be at the doughnut shop across the road complaining about the job, as they usually did at this early hour of the morning. Anywhere in the world would be preferable to where he was, stuck inside some hellish nightmare, separated from Angelo and trying to save the world. At the thought of Angelo, Ray's mind snapped back into focus.

"Mr Mitchell?"

The man did not respond, but remained staring out the window.

"Mr Mitchell. You're under arrest for the murder of that fifteen-year-old girl back along the corridor. Get down on your knees and put your hands behind your head."

Mitchell turned and locked eyes with Ray. "Hey, Bro, how ya doin?" he crooned, a grin spreading across his fat face.

Ray's mouth fell open in shock. "What the fuck? I said get down on your knees." He held his gun towards Mitchell's chest, the flashlight still balanced along the barrel.

"I enjoyed fucking Christy Merle y'know. She was a real sweet ride, made all the more sweet for having taken her from you, little brother."

"What the fuck is going on?" Ray hissed, his eyes wide in shock as he listened to Mitchell's taunts.

"How long has it been huh, twenty years since I left home to join the marines? You haven't seen me in all those years and you don't even recognise your own brother."

"You're a sicko," Ray spat. "Your name's Mitchell. You live in apartment one two seven on the twenty second floor. You play dungeons and dragons and you've probably not been laid in years. How the fuck do you know about my brother, or Christy Merle?"

"Look at me, Ray, take a close look." Mitchell took a step towards him and leaned forward slightly; holding Ray's eyes with his own intense stare. Ray examined his face; saw the double chin and fleshy cheeks, the dark brown eyes and acne scarred forehead. As he looked, Mitchell's face changed. The flesh squirmed, came alive and moved across the supporting bones beneath before settling once again. As Mitchell's face disappeared, Ray looked into his older brother's eyes and gasped.

"Chris?" He whispered as he continued gazing.

"I took her from you because you were not man enough for her. She liked it rough, little brother, and boy did I give her what she craved. We used to laugh, she and I. We would laugh at the thought of little Ray being so in love with her. You stupid little fool, you'd only just learned to masturbate, what in the world made you believe you could satisfy a lustful woman like Christy Merle?"

"That's not true," Ray countered, desperately trying to make sense of this craziness, to find some order amongst the chaos that his mind would be able to hold on to.

Mitchell grimaced with anger as he took a couple more steps towards Ray. "It's true, asshole, and you know it. All those years you couldn't face me because you knew I was the man you wanted to be. You punished me for being everything you wanted to be but couldn't."

"Shut the fuck up," Ray yelled, spittle flying out of his mouth. "I loved Christy and she was going to be my girl when you came and took her away. She was beautiful, sweet, and kind until you came along and made her into a cruel slut. You were made for each other, the asshole and the whore, and I've not missed either of you for a minute."

"You lie," Mitchell yelled back, pointing at Ray to push his point. "You've thought of nothing else in the entire twenty years since that day you weren't even man enough to push me off the roof." He stopped yelling and grinned as Ray's mouth fell open in surprise. He nodded slowly, his eyes never leaving Ray's. "You've never forgiven me for taking Christy have you, little Bro? It's only the desire for revenge that's kept you going when you wake up in the early hours, alone and afraid. Well now's your chance, little man. Now you can finally pay me back for taking that whore from you. Go on, you've wanted nothing else for twenty years. Do it now, little Bro, show me you're man enough to pay me back."

Tears coursed down Ray's cheeks as he stared at the man before him. "You didn't take the whore from me. You took a sweet girl who liked me and turned her into a whore. You're not Chris, you're not my brother. He always called her 'that sweet little thing who fancies Ray' whenever he spoke about her. Even after he took her from me, he still called her 'that funny little virgin.' He never called her a whore. It's me that calls her that name. Chris would never say that. Now get down on your knees."

Mitchell growled in anger, balling his fists and staring at Ray as the apparition of Chris's face disappeared. Ray watched as the double chin, fleshy cheeks, and acne scars returned. He was so distracted by the strangeness of it that he failed to react in time as Mitchell closed the distance between them and lunged for the gun. Caught unawares, Ray was unable to prevent Mitchell from wrenching the gun from his grasp and fell to his knees as he realised he was about to die. He was determined not to die while subject to some evil thing, and let his mind go inwards as he waited for the end. Angelo sprang into his mind first, and Ray felt genuine love for his partner and friend. "I'm sorry I can't be there to help you, Angelo. You're my best friend. Thank you for everything." The next face that came to his mind was that of his older brother Chris, and he cried for the wasted years of hatred between them.

Four shots rang out and Ray jumped in surprise. Opening his eyes, he saw Mitchell, gun still held against what remained of his skull, the unmistakeable smell of blood and gunfire filling his nostrils. Mitchell's body crumpled, coming to rest a few feet in front of Ray, who jumped back in alarm, not wanting to come into contact with any of the mushy remains. The gun slid across the wooden floor and came to rest against the leg of the glass coffee table with an audible clink. For several seconds Ray knelt, breathing hard as he tried to recover from the shock of the situation. Finally, he shook his head and stood, walked across the room and retrieved his gun before heading towards the door.

The air was heavy outside in the corridor and the smell, overpowering. Sticky black ooze flowed down the walls and puddled on the floor. Ray gagged and vomited as he stumbled along the corridor. Thoughts raced through his mind as he struggled along, and he fought to put them into some order. Highest on his list of priority was helping Angelo. He would be downstairs by now, he remembered, and on his way to apartment seventy to destroy the portal. Next came anger, and lots of it, unbidden and terrifying in its intensity. Twenty years of living with unexpressed anger came boiling up. The years of living with the grief of losing Christy Merle to someone he looked up to and admired crawled up from the black depths of his heart. The death of his friendship with his brother, and his subsequent difficulties relating to women, all of it and more came flooding to the surface and out as he screamed in anguish. The distant sound of gunfire caught his attention and he knew he must reach Angelo soon or all would be lost. The anger, loneliness and fear coursed through him as he fought his way through the wretched smell and rivers of black sticky ooze. He was angry at what Chris had done all those years ago, but he was also angry with himself for being so hurt and keeping everything locked away. There was anger at Christy Merle for having allowed it to happen, knowing how much the young Ray had loved her. Twenty years of loneliness, during which he was too afraid to get involved again for fear of losing again, came back in a rush. The years of being afraid of hurting that much ever again caused Ray to cry aloud in anger. There were two things that held his mind together, getting to Angelo, and the anger. As he descended the stairs, Ray's strength of mind faltered under the weight of his anguish.

31

Outside, several police cars had blocked the street. Their occupants were taking cover behind their vehicles as chaos reigned all around them. The violence that apparently erupted outside the entrance to Gainsford House had now spread down the sidewalk a little. Curious faces peered out from windows of the apartments above the stores and offices either side. All of them worried for their own buildings as they watched the enraged crowd below trying desperately to gain access. An hour and ten minutes before, two men had drawn guns and shot randomly until they were both out of ammunition. One of them had been carrying a spare clip, which he used to shoot his fellow gunman, before continuing his volley into the crowd that was by now running screaming in all directions. When the police arrived, he shot two officers and wounded several more before they too took cover. Then he turned his attention to shooting out the door to the men's outfitters and bespoke tailoring service that operated in the building on one side of Gainsford House.

There were several floors of offices above the men's outfitters, but also three apartments, and it was these to which the gunman ran. As he made his way through the building, he was too consumed with the drive to cause mayhem to notice the black liquid that now oozed from the walls and trickled down to the floor. By the time he reached the first of the three apartments, he found the two residents dead and dismembered, victims of their own compassion as they answered the frantic knock at their door and found one of their neighbours standing there with an axe. The second apartment was empty, and the third looked like a hurricane had swept through. Chairs and tables lay smashed, testament to a sudden and unimaginable violence that not only tore the rooms limb from limb, but also tainted the atmosphere with foreboding. The single resident, a middle-aged man who managed the men's outfitters below, had been awake and taking a pee when he noticed something was wrong. Hearing the screams from the apartment next door as his colleagues John Henry and Finian Pickings begged for their lives, he ran for his own life down the stairs and through the shop to the street. Flinging open the side door after fumbling for the key he kept hidden in the coffee jar in the staff kitchen, he ran up the narrow alley to the street. He surged forwards at the sight of the flashing red and blue of the police cars, like beacons of safety on a dark night they beckoned to him. On reaching the sidewalk at the front of the building, he barely registered the raised voices and commotion. His attention remained solidly fixed on the police cars he saw parked on the opposite sidewalk. Screaming in terror, he held out his arms, beseeching the officers as he raced towards them. A crack split the air and he noticed a pain in his chest that took the breath from his lungs. Before darkness overtook him, he lifted his head from the ground and noticed a cop standing up behind the trunk of one of the police cars, his arms still held out in front to steady his aim.

On the other side of Gainsford House was a general store at ground level, with three floors of offices above, and four more floors of apartments above that. Chaos was already taking hold amongst the residents, all of whom were either consumed with the need for violence, or dead as a result of conflicts with other residents. As each person succumbed to the dark energy and let their own violent natures out from the restraints placed there by societal mores, the darkness spread a little further. Everywhere the darkness was, violence and chaos ensued. The buildings and the earth itself throbbed with menace, the tangible sense of evil heavy in the air. Black ooze flowed everywhere from unseen pores, a physical manifestation of the unseen controlling force that as yet, so few knew existed. Within minutes the process of decomposition began, the smell flowing on the breeze into everyone's nostrils, making them gag and vomit.

"What the fuck is that smell?" a police officer asked from the cover of his vehicle.

"I've no idea but it's making me sick," his colleague replied, then hunched over to his left and vomited onto the sidewalk. Holding his stomach as waves of nausea flowed through him, the officer groaned aloud as griping pains sliced across his abdomen. Calling for help did no good, for many of his colleagues were in the same predicament, as was everyone who smelled that black rotting ooze. The sounds of gunfire and screaming from all directions went unheeded as the officers fell victim to that smell, a distasteful but deadly precursor to the further horror that awaited them. As if in a waking sleep, the officers lay on the ground, aware but unable to move, held captive by the sedative effect of the aroma from the malodorous black ooze. Terrified beyond their worst nightmares, they lay and waited for the dark force to gain enough strength to spread far enough to reach them. Gradually, the circle of darkness crept out from Gainsford House in all directions, a slow and steady progression of violence and descent into chaos. The people themselves fuelled this engine of horror as they willingly tore down the barriers between the standards expected of the society in which they live, and their natural violent natures.

On the twelfth floor stairwell, Angelo and Nessy peered through the small window into the corridor. Angelo snapped his head back and yanked Nessy down into a crouch behind the door.

"Shit. Shit and fuck."

"What?"

"Someone's there right outside what must be Harlon Drake's front door."

"Who is it?"

"I don't know, a guy. It looks like he's murdering someone. I saw him beating at something on the floor. I only saw for a second."

"So there's only one person?" Nessy asked and Angelo nodded.

"As far as I can see yeah. We don't know if anyone is in the apartment though, and we have to gain access first. I can pick the lock but it will take a minute. How are you with a gun?"

"Oh heaven's no, I couldn't," she replied immediately and Angelo silently cursed.

"Any idea when your spirit friend is going to help us out here? She's been full of advice but so far little actual assistance. We're on our own here y'know. Ray has left us and no doubt is lost to the thing, whatever it is, and I only have half a magazine of ammunition left. I can't hold out for long and what do I use for protection then huh, harsh language?"

"Please don't panic, not at this stage," Nessy soothed. "You can panic and yell later okay? I give you my word I will let you yell at me and won't yell back, once this is finished. Right now though, we both need you to hold it together."

"I'm sorry," Angelo said. "Ray's been my partner since we both joined the police and I can't go and help him. What do you think that does to me huh? He's my best friend and I have to leave him to suffer and turn into something crazy. That goes against everything I believe in, and I'm sorry if my emotions are inconvenient to you."

"They're not inconvenient at all," she replied. "Come on, follow me." She stood and yanked open the door, striding through into the corridor.

"What the fuck?" Angelo screeched and ran after her. "Lady, do you have a death wish?

"How do you feel about letting Ray go off on his own?" Nessy asked aloud. "Tell me about it, Angelo; tell me about it right now." Up ahead, the man who sat astride the now dead woman looked round, his arms held aloft in mid stroke, the blood dripping from his fists. Below him, the woman's head was almost flat, except for two spikes of skull bone that stuck up from where they had been smashed, while lumps of brain matter lay strewn around him in a circle two metres in diameter. Angelo swallowed hard as the man got to his feet, his mouth spreading into a rictus that he guessed was the nearest the guy could get to a malicious sneer. He was vaguely aware of Nessy yelling at him as the man came towards them, his mouth issuing forth an unearthly growling snarl. Red-hot pain slashed across his face and Angelo looked down at Nessy, her hand readied for another slap.

"I said tell me about Ray. How do you feel about leaving him huh? Does it upset you, Angelo?" He frowned, and was about to question her when he remembered their conversation earlier. She had explained before they set out that keeping compassion and love strong in their hearts and minds would be as effective a source of protection as would the bullets in his gun.

"Oh," he exclaimed, his eyes widening as the true meaning of her words sank in. He closed his eyes and filled his mind with the memory of Ray leaving them upstairs. He allowed his anguish for his friend's safety to fill his heart and overflow down his cheeks as he dwelt upon the bond they enjoyed. Looking at the crazed man that still approached them, Angelo let his heart fill with emotion and stream down his cheeks. The man reacted instantly, holding his arms across his face as if to protect himself from a naked flame. With a yell of surprise and fear, the man stumbled back down the corridor and away.

"Come on," Nessy hissed and grabbed his arm. "We must get into the apartment before he comes back and before any more get here. The thing knows what we're trying to do now, and it will send the people under its control to try to stop us. We'll have a mob on our backs anytime soon. Hurry please."

"Thanks, and I'm sorry for losing my temper just now," Angelo sniffed as he wiped his eyes and fumbled for his lock pick.

"I forgive you," she replied and squeezed his arm. "You get on with breaking in and I'll keep watch."

He nodded and looked at the door. "It's already open." Nessy frowned and he shrugged. Taking hold of his gun, he raised the flashlight and kicked the door. It flew in and banged against the wall behind, the noise making Nessy jump. After swinging the flashlight around and finding the hallway empty, they leapt inside and shut the door behind them.

"Now what?" he asked. Nessy's mouth flapped as she reddened. "Come on, baby, don't flake on me now huh?" he soothed. "Where's Patty and what does she want us to do? Can you maybe talk to her or something? Now would be a great time for some help or advice."

"Well I err," she began.

"Don't panic, just close your eyes and ask for her, or whatever it is that you do."

Nessy closed her eyes. What seemed like hours later, she opened them again. "She says to remember the love."

"What? Is that all?" Angelo almost cried.

"Yeah," Nessy nodded.

"Love won't help you now," the voice cut in before Angelo replied. Nessy spun around, startled by the knowledge that someone was behind her, and Angelo looked up into the familiar face of his partner Ray, who stood in the open doorway to the hall bathroom.

"Ray?" Angelo cried out in relief. "Buddy, I was so worried about you." He moved towards him then noticed the gun in his partner's hand, the gun that was now pointed at him and stopped in his tracks as his heart fell. "Oh no. Ray, please not you too."

"We can't let you do this. The portal must be protected for the others to come through and finish the cleansing."

"Cleansing?" Angelo hoped that by engaging him in conversation, it would give him the time and opportunity to disarm him. He was not hopeful, as Ray had always been the better marksman of them both, and Angelo had to accept that he might not get out of this alive.

"This world has become poisoned and must be cleansed. You humans and your toxic emotions have all but choked the life from this dimension, but everything is all right now, for the master is here to cleanse it and save it."

"What do you mean toxic emotions?" Angelo asked.

"Never mind that," Ray snapped, his mouth now a thin angry line. "We cannot allow you to destroy the portal, and you must become one with the master"

175

"Remember the love, Angelo," Nessy whispered and Angelo's mind raced as he grasped Patty's message at last.

"Shut up you disgusting filth," Ray said and glared at Nessy.

"Remember the love, Angelo," she repeated. Angelo squeezed her shoulder in an attempt to quieten her. He did not want her to provoke Ray any further.

"We said be quiet," Ray screamed, snapping his arm around and firing. Nessy gasped in shock as her head flew back, blood spattering Angelo's cheek, before crumpling into his arms.

"No," Angelo screamed as he caught Nessy and lowered her to the floor. He looked up at Ray as anger flashed through his mind. At the same moment, he saw the trace of a smile find Ray's lips and his head nod in approval, a tiny movement at the corners. Thoughts raced through his mind, all jumbled and without the order necessary to form a coherent plan. Nessy lay at his feet, her eyes wide and her mouth moving silently, and Angelo was aware of many emotions. On the one hand, he was sad at her dying like this, while trying to help him save everyone from something indescribably awful. He had not known her more than a few hours but they had bonded despite their short friendship, and he knew he would mourn her passing. On the other hand, he was angry with Ray. He was angry with him for leaving them, for letting the thing into his head and for going crazy like the others. Most of all he was angry with him for shooting Nessy, who only wanted to help them both. He looked into her eyes as they held his gaze and bent down to kiss her cheek.

"The love, Angelo. Remember," she whispered as her eyes closed.

A noise caught Angelo's attention and cut through his train of angry thoughts. The stairwell door was opening with a creak, and the baying of the crowd was now deafening. Angelo knew they were just yards from the door and felt a flutter of panic course through his veins. He buried his head in Nessy's neck, trying to blot out the horror so he could concentrate on his emotions. One thought came to the front of his mind stronger than any other, and he held onto it with all of his mental strength. He missed his friend.

"Ray." He stood and allowed the tears to run freely down his cheeks. "I miss you. I miss our friendship. The laughter, the jokes and the jibes. I want you back, man. You're my best friend, don't leave me now, I need you."

"Stop," Ray said, the smile falling from his lips as he blinked nervously. The gun in his hands shook as hesitation momentarily took hold. "We must," he began but faltered. "It's not," he tried again, and then dropped his eyes to the floor in panic.

Angelo kept up the onslaught. "We've been best friends forever haven't we? Theresa loves you like a brother, hell I love you like a brother. Come on, don't desert me now. I want my friend back, I miss you.

"Stop," Ray whispered, his face grimacing as if in physical pain. He hunched over, the gun falling to the floor at his feet as he cried out and held his head. "I can't, we have to," he tried again but failed as Angelo leapt at him and grabbed him in a bear hug.

"Come back to me, please. I need you, you're my best friend. Please help me; you're the only one I can trust."

"Angelo?"

"Yeah, it's me," He grinned and let his friend loose from the hug. "Welcome back. Are you with me?"

"What happened?"

"I'll tell you all about it later. Right now, I need you with me okay? We have an angry mob descending on us and I can't do this alone. Are you up to a fight?"

"Yeah, of course. Where's Nessy?"

Angelo stepped aside so Ray could see her body. Ray gasped, put a hand to his mouth and cried out. His body shook as he tried to control the sobs.

"I thought I dreamed it," he whispered when he could speak.

"Do you feel bad about it?" Angelo asked and hated himself for asking.

"Of course, why ask me that?"

"Hold that strong in your mind okay? Remember what Nessy said earlier? Feel the love? Keep that with you, don't leave me again huh?"

"Okay," Ray sniffed and nodded. Taking up his gun, he checked the magazine and found several bullets missing. Knowing the horrific images he thought were a nightmare were in fact real, he did not fight the guilt that flowed through him.

"Where's the portal thing?" Angelo asked. "The mirror."

"It's in the closet over there." Ray indicated a door halfway down the short hallway.

"Okay," Angelo said and raced towards the door. Yanking it open, he saw the huge black framed mirror on the wall inside, an imposing feature that reminded him of all those black and white Victorian movies Theresa loves so much. It was ugly, gave him the creeps and he would be happy to destroy it.

"We're supposed to wait until the thing goes back through," Ray said.

"Yeah but how do we achieve that now that Nessy's dead?" Before Ray could shrug his shoulders, the front door flew open and the crowd burst in.

32

It was strong, and getting stronger with each passing hour. The humans were succumbing easily and providing more than enough negative energy upon which It could feed and grow. The building containing the portal was now impenetrable and It could now concentrate on those either side. If this dimension were to be cleansed properly, It would need to move further beyond the portal and extend itself. The stronger It became, the quicker the humans allowed themselves to be influenced, the faster they conceded control. This dimension was strange, much more chaotic than the dimension It knew as home, but chaotic in a bad way. The chaos was half-heartedly wrought and the precious negative energies were quickly spent then hidden away in shame. The society under whose rule the humans lived frowned upon negativity and punishments were often extreme for those who allowed their true nature to express itself for too long. There was too much control of the wrong kind in this dimension, and It knew that the humans would be only too willing to embrace this new liberation from the stifling constraints of their social morality.

Suddenly, the energies changed and It focussed on Gainsford House. It probed the corridors and rooms, stairwells and halls, and quickly realised that three people were out to destroy It and the great cleansing. How the three had gained entry to the building without being discovered before, It did not know, but now that it was aware, they would not survive long. Linking to the minds of all the humans within the building, It gave the order to destroy these troublesome interlopers. All over Gainsford House, the people stopped, cocked their heads to the side as if listening to something, then turned round and headed towards the stairs. There was great danger on the twelfth floor, and three people must be killed in order to prevent a disaster.

Not long later, It felt one of the interlopers succumb to the dark energy and although unable to exhibit any form of human emotion, It knew this event was of benefit. It knew that the humans under control would deal with the other two, if they did not succumb to the dark influence first. It resumed its task of extending itself, growing into the neighbouring buildings with ease. It spread across the street to the other side and across the alley at the rear to the buildings behind. Like a slow motion tidal wave, the dark influence spread in all directions, with It controlling at the centre, feeding upon the negative emotions, chaos, and violence given off by the humans under Its influence. Wherever It touched a human mind, that human changed and chaos ensued. People were rioting in the streets for six city blocks around Gainsford House. Neighbour killed neighbour, parents attacked children, and stranger murdered stranger. The black ooze came first, and with it the foul aroma to sedate the body and mind while It wove its dark magic and brought the barriers built by generations of social rules crashing down. The police who had been stricken by the effect of that deadly fume, quickly joined the chaos, and bodies now littered the sidewalks. They roamed the buildings, shooting anything that moved, even each other, and brought New York to a standstill.

It swelled with renewed strength as this cleansing took place, a small beginning that would, ultimately, see the entire dimension cleansed of the toxic and fetid poison leached from the minds of the humans. The compassion, joy, love and need to create life had slowly but surely brought this dimension to its knees, and It intended to rectify this disaster. These humans had been left uncontrolled for too long. Left to themselves, they quickly put away their true savage nature and allowed social moralities to poison their world. It redoubled its work, and was determined to cleanse the poison from every inch of this dimension, no matter how long it took. Suddenly, It knew there was terrible danger and stopped what It was doing. Every human under Its control was aware too and stopped, silent, waiting. The portal, it was in danger. There was a strong smell of a poisonous and positive energy source nearby, and It knew the danger that now threatened. Although It was now strong in this dimension and would succeed with the cleansing, a way back to its own dimension must always be available. Knowing that there was terrible danger, It flew back to the portal.

33

Angelo and Ray stood side by side in the hallway of apartment seventy and opened fire as the baying crowd rushed in. Even with both of them firing, they were soon overwhelmed and the last thing Angelo did before falling to the floor and waiting for the end was to pray.

"Oh God, please help us."

"I'm sorry, Angelo," Ray yelled. "I love you, man."

"I forgive you," he yelled back. "I love you too."

"Only those who are pure of heart may enter herein," the female voice boomed. The hallway exploded into light and Angelo raised his hands to shield his eyes. Peering through his fingers, he saw Nessy, or something that looked like her, floating a couple of feet off the ground and surrounded by a dazzling white light that filled the hallway.

"Nessy?" he said. He looked to where her body still lay, then back to the dazzling form that floated in front of him.

Ray frowned. "But it can't be her, she's dead. Her body is still on the floor, look," he said and pointed. Angelo nodded and shrugged. The bodies of those killed by the two police officers' bullets lay everywhere, and around them, cowering in terror, were those of the baying crowd who still survived. Those who had not yet managed to gain entry to the apartment had fled away down the corridors and stairs. They hoped that if they put distance between themselves and the terrible light, they would be safe.

"Our world is a place of both extremes, and all the wonderful nuances in between," the shimmering shade who looked like Nessy continued. "There can be no anger without peace, no hate without love, no darkness without light. Neither one can overpower the other, for to do so would unbalance us. It is the way of the universe my friends. Both must be nurtured in their own way, but neither allowed to dominate."

"Nessy?" Ray said as he stood and looked at the dazzling form. "It is you. I'm so sorry for what I did to you. The thing, it got inside my mind and I couldn't resist it. Please believe me. I would never want to harm you." Angelo saw his friend crying with shame and his heart became heavy with sadness for him. He put a hand on his shoulder and squeezed.

"Without your action," the shade that both firmly believed was Nessy, replied, "we would not be able to end this torment that threatens our world. You made this possible. Do not feel shame."

"I don't understand," Ray frowned.

"I think she means this was the only way she could help end this," Angelo said. "She knew there was only one way to do this. She knew she had to die to kill this thing. Without your shot, she wouldn't be in a position to help us now."

"Why did I have to kill her?" Ray wailed as tears streamed down his cheeks. "Why couldn't she do it without dying? I killed her, Angelo, how do I live with that huh? I know we're cops but I never killed an innocent woman before." Angelo held him as he wailed into his chest. He looked up at Nessy and saw her nod slowly. He nodded back.

"Ouch, what was that?" Ray asked suddenly, his head snapping up from Angelo's chest. Angelo put his hands to his ears and winced.

"I don't know but my ears hurt," he replied.

"Mine too."

The air inside the hallway stirred, a gentle breeze at first that swelled to become a raging hurricane. The entire building seemed to be vibrating. The picture of a sailing ship that hung on the wall rattled on its hook and fell to the floor with a clonk. From all around them, they heard the sounds of doors banging, only the bodies piled inside the front door preventing the one before them from joining in. The noise that hurt their ears so, that was at first above the level of human hearing, became an audible roar that reverberated along the corridors and down the stairwells and lift shafts. Angelo and Ray looked towards Nessy, their hands covering their ears but still the noise was painful. The iridescent angelic forms joined her from some other, unknown realm and stood with her, side by side in their thousands. It did not occur to either of them at the time how so many could fit in the confined space of the hallway at once, and they gazed transfixed at the sight. The dazzling light fell upon the mirror and Angelo would swear until the day he died that he saw the surface move like liquid for a split second.

The roaring intensified, the hurricane strengthened and the two men fell to the floor to prevent themselves from being blown over. The small hall table came flying towards them and caught Angelo a glancing blow on his left elbow. He howled in pain and cowered with Ray in the far corner of the small closet, opposite the huge imposing mirror. The legion of dazzling angelic forms raised their voices and let forth a sound, a note of such pure quality neither man had ever heard, nor ever would again, and they saw the darkness rushing towards the mirror and right through it as if the glass was not there.

As the dark being fled towards the portal, the humans who seconds ago had been under its complete control, found themselves abandoned. As their own minds flew from their imprisonment, many broke under the strain, the delicate brain chemistry and wiring of the neurones forever destroyed by the presence of the dark being. Some stood silent, unable to comprehend anything, whilst others wandered around bemused at the carnage around them. A few dropped dead the moment the dark being left them, their minds simply too injured to sustain life without it. Many, remembering what they had done during the strange experience, wept in shame and anguish. Angelo saw and heard the dark being fight briefly with the angelic throng, but one shard of the dazzling white light on the surface of the mirror sent it screaming back from whence it came. For a moment, the surface of the mirror was black, unable to reflect anything and the two men stared into the black depths of a dimension they had no business seeing. All at once the blackness was gone, and their reflections gazed back at them, the mirror just a mirror once again.

Cradling his painful elbow gently, Angelo stepped out of the closet, stepping over bodies as carefully as he could. Ray followed and together they stood and watched as the angelic throng crowded around the mirror.

"What are they doing?" Ray said.

"I've no idea but I hope they're fixing it so the thing can't come back."

"Is it really over?"

"The dark one is gone," the dazzling form of Nessy replied as she hovered in mid-air and gazed at them. "We must ensure that this portal is forever closed. Stand back now and shield yourselves, quickly." They turned and shielded themselves as the mirror exploded within the closet, its remains now nothing but fine dust that glinted like Christmas glitter. No one would ever be able to repair that.

Angelo nodded. "Thank you so much. What the hell can I say when you've sacrificed yourself. Thank you is inadequate."

"The sacrifice was not that great," she replied. "I have helped save the world. How many people can boast of that?"

"Certainly not me," Ray said. "I know you don't agree, but I feel terrible for what I did. I know you said it was necessary but I can't be okay with having shot someone in cold blood like that. I will gladly accept my punishment."

"There will be no punishment my friend," Nessy replied, "for you didn't kill me."

"But," Ray frowned and looked at Angelo, to find him frowning too. Nessy's dazzling shade was now gone and the light extinguished. The hallway was dark after the brightness that they had become used to, and all was silent save for the distant sound of wailing sirens from the street outside. Nessy's body still lay on the floor.

"But I did kill her," Ray said.

"She died in my arms," Angelo nodded.

"Maybe she meant I didn't kill her because her spirit still lives on."

"That's it," Angelo nodded. "That has to be it." They walked over to her and crouched down. Ray put his hand on her shoulder as hot tears stung his eyes. Angelo looked at her head wound and frowned. There was a lot of blood, which hid the truth from their eyes. The bullet had hit her and glanced off.

"Hey, look," he said, grabbing Ray's shoulder. "Hey, look," he yelled.

"What?" Ray said wiping his eyes.

"Your shot caught her a glancing blow to the temple. It hit but glanced off somewhere. Your bullet is probably embedded in that wall beside the front door. A moment of silence passed between them before Ray shook his head and looked back down at Nessy.

"No, I uh, I can't," he whispered.

"What would Nessy say?" Angelo replied.

"Probably the same as you're suggesting."

"Hey I'm not suggesting anything. I'm simply reporting that you fired your weapon and the bullet caught this woman a glancing blow to the temple in the craziness that was going down here in this dark and confined space. That's all I'm saying, and it happens to be the truth."

"Yeah I know, and I appreciate it but I," Ray began but a small noise caught their attention. They listened and it came again, a small moan.

"Nessy?" Angelo said and touched her neck. "Nessy? Shit, she has a pulse. Come on; help me get her out of here so we can call for help."

Between them, Angelo and Ray got Nessy out of Gainsford House and used the radio in Ray's vandalised car to call for an ambulance. Until he gave his police badge number, the operator tried to tell him it would be a long wait, due to the horrific riot that had taken place in that area. Once Nessy was made comfortable in the back seat of the car. Angelo and Ray looked around and were shocked at the scene. They saw a police officer stumbling around as if drunk and sat him down.

"What happened out here?" Angelo asked. The officer shook his head and ran a hand through his hair.

"Everyone went crazy. We got the call that a murder had taken place on the street here, and that the gunman was still around making threats. When we got here, there was a crowd of people over by Gainsford House going nuts. Two of them brought out guns and one shot the other, then started shooting at random. We got behind the vehicles and then there was this awful smell. After that, it's as if I was having a nightmare, but it was more vivid than a nightmare. It was like I was really there y'know? I did things, we did things, all of the officers that were with me out here, we just lost it. We were shooting each other, and random people we saw in the street. Then I suddenly wake up from this nightmare and find bodies all around me. How the fuck do I deal with this?"

"Don't try," Angelo said. "At least not right now. Concentrate on recovering for now. It was a bad dream, hold onto that huh?"

"Do you have any water?" the officer asked. Both men went to check the police cars for a bottle and left the officer sitting on the kerb. Before either of them found any water, the shot rang out in the deserted street and both jumped around. The officer had shot himself through the head; his body now sprawled into the road. How many other officers would find it too hard to cope with their memories? Angelo suddenly worried for Ray.

The clean-up began the next morning, which was no more than a couple of hours away and the two men travelled to the hospital with Nessy, before heading back to the precinct to see who was left. Only six officers from their precinct were involved, the majority who got the call were not known to either Angelo or Ray. The total number of deaths was eventually recorded at one hundred and eighty seven, including twenty-four police officers, most of whom had shot each other. Subsequent forensic testing showed that only four members of the public were shot by police officers, all of whom were too busy fighting amongst themselves to take too much notice of what was going on around them.

Harlon Drake was discovered in the stairwell of Gainsford House, naked and bleeding from multiple beatings. He was unable to speak, and no amount of questioning got anything from him. He spent every waking minute looking down at his hands, rocking back and forth, and spitting into his lap. He was doubly incontinent, and would sit in his own mess rather than get up and use the toilet in his hospital room. He was admitted to a secure psychiatric facility where he could be cared for by dedicated nurses and doctors. The place was well known for providing a loving and nurturing environment for those with psychiatric illnesses, the sale of his apartment and all of his belongings, together with the contents of his bank account, ensuring the best of care for the rest of his life.

Both Angelo and Ray went through the appropriate procedure when it became apparent that they had fired their weapons, but they were not found to be guilty of any misconduct. It quickly became apparent that those who had been acting violently and who had recovered from it, had some chemical changes within their brains, and it was used as a marker to find out who had been the crazies and who were not. These changes were found in all of the victims Angelo and Ray had shot, so it was recorded in the file that they both fired their weapons in self-defence. Both were later awarded the NYPD Medal of Honour, when it became known that they were in the thick of it inside Gainsford House for the duration.

Angelo sat in Nessy Bellinger's living room and sipped the tea she made. Ray bit into the delicious cake she offered and nodded appreciatively. She was out of hospital within a week with a clean bill of health and was smiling.

"How are you, Nessy?" Angelo asked.

"I'm great, thank you. And I do mean that. I am great."

"That's wonderful," Ray said. "I'm so happy you're back to your normal self again so quickly."

"Well not entirely my normal self," she said and both men frowned. "I've lost my gift."

"You have?" Angelo said and she nodded.

"Yes. When I was unconscious, after we had got rid of that thing, Patty told me some things that made everything clear."

"Can you share them with us?" Ray asked.

"Of course. She told me that this was the reason I was given the gift at birth, that it was my destiny. Once I had fulfilled my destiny, they took it away so I can live a normal life."

"You didn't live a normal life before?" Angelo asked.

"No. It was impossible. Whenever in the company of people, their deceased relatives and friends would be hounding me to pass on messages. It was never ending. I had to become something of a recluse in order to get a little peace. Now I can join the human race and have friends, start dating maybe. I already have a job I enjoy but I can now try and find a social life at least."

"Of course you can," Ray said. "You can start by letting me take you out for a drink. I have some friends I can introduce you to, and that will get your social life started."

"That's a great idea, thank you."

"Did Patty tell you anything more about the thing?" Angelo asked. "What it is and where it came from? She told us when we first met you that we created it out of our own negative thoughts and emotions, but what exactly was it, and how did we create it?"

"It's not some creature from another planet or dimension, and it's not and evil demon or anything of that nature. It's a product of human emotion, the negative emotions like anger, fear, and the want of cruelty. We made it, us humans made it and we will continue to make it. Every time we display anger, hatred, and fear and every time we willingly hurt someone or be cruel, we're making it stronger. The negative energy of those thoughts and actions don't simply dissipate into the air, they collect, attracted by the presence of others like themselves. Over time, the accumulation of all that negativity, hate, and cruelty, becomes aware, becomes alive and takes on a purpose unique to itself."

"What about the portal?" Ray asked. "What part does that play if this is made from us humans?"

"As a being of pure negative energy, it cannot survive amongst us where we have other, more positive emotions like joy and love. Those positive emotions are its polar opposite, and unless they are in balance, one side will cancel the other out. That's why it ran from all positivity, and why I kept telling you to keep that positivity in the front of your hearts and minds. There are many dimensions within our universe, too many to count, and once this thing becomes aware of its own existence and takes on a purpose, it dwells in another of these dimensions where it can be sure there is no human positivity. Being made from human emotional energy, it has an unbreakable tie with humans and will always be pulled to the human dimension. The portal is how it travels between dimensions. Having no physical body means it can travel between dimensions easily."

"So it might come back one day?" Angelo said.

"Yes, it could. If it finds another portal and someone willing to open it."

"Like Harlon Drake."

"Yes. He used the mirror in an effort to achieve spirit communication with his ancestor Patricia Drake, but got a bit more than he bargained for. The thing, having got inside his mind, knew of his desire to communicate with her, so it pretended to be her spirit to ensure his compliance."

"How the hell do we make sure that there's not too much negativity?" Ray said. "This is New York y'know. Murders happen here every day. Stick ups, car jackings, beatings, muggings and all sorts of other shit. We're doomed."

"Believe me, for every act of cruelty there is one of love," Nessy said. "This is a big world we live in, and even here in New York, wonderful acts of love happen every day too. Just because you don't witness them, doesn't mean they don't happen. You're cops; you only see the bad stuff."

Ray nodded. "I'm delighted to hear that."

"Those other beings," Angelo said quietly. "The ones we saw with you. They were uh, there were so many. Thousands of them. They looked like uh, well, y'know. Did we imagine that?"

"You didn't imagine it," she replied and emotion swelled in his heart. Before he had time to take a breath, he was sobbing and Nessy took hold of his hand.

Ray reached out and squeezed his shoulder. "What's up?"

"Before you and the uh," Angelo hesitated. "Well, before they disappeared, one of them stepped towards me for a split second and I saw a little girl holding hands with him. He never said anything but I knew that the little girl was Anna Marie. She was perfect, and so beautiful. I wish Theresa could've seen it."

"She doesn't need to see it," Nessy replied. "She already knows in her heart and her belief had never wavered. You saw because you needed to see." Angelo said nothing, but nodded as he wiped his eyes.

"I'm glad you told me that," Ray replied, "cos it makes me feel less foolish when I tell you that one of them told me something."

"Yeah?" Angelo said, sniffing.

"Yeah. Like you said, he didn't say it with his mouth, but I heard it inside my head and his voice just made me believe instantly. He said not to give up on love because it waits for me just around the corner."

"That's awesome," Angelo grinned.

"I hope it's true."

"If they told you, then you can believe it," Nessy replied.

Angelo Lamora took his wife Theresa on a slightly delayed holiday to the Dominican Republic, where they relaxed, swam a lot, and made love with renewed passion. Ray took a couple of weeks off and went to visit his parents. He found his brother there and over the space of the two weeks, they destroyed the aching void that had come between them. Both Angelo and Ray returned to work renewed and ready to start again. One day, when things had calmed from what had become known as The Gainsford Riot, Ray called over to Ted Fancourt, where he sat on the opposite side of the office.

"I want to apologise to you for accusing you last year. It was wrong and I'm sorry." Silence gripped the room as everyone waited for Ted's reply. He had been consumed with anger at Ray for accusing him, and had vowed never to speak to him again. This public apology, although late, had caught him unawares and for long seconds he did not know how to respond.

Two minutes later, they shook hands and Ray was relieved. Angelo grinned and clapped him on the back.

"Well done, I'm proud of you, man."

Harlon Drake lay on his bed and stared at his hands. The nurse had recently cleaned up the mess he had made in the bed and now he lay waiting for sleep. The nurses were kind and left the light on for him at night, knowing that if left in the dark, he would howl for hours. Nothing occupied his mind as he waited for sleep; he simply waited and looked at his hands. Suddenly, a voice caught his attention and despite the void inside what used to be his mind, he looked up to find a beautiful brunette standing beside his bed. She was smiling and seemed nice.

"Hello Harlon. My name is Patricia Drake but everyone calls me Patty."

THE END

COMING SOON

We all have dirty little secrets, don't we?

When Sam Sinclair is called home to help solve the murder of a fellow law enforcer, he comes to question what might lie within the darkest recesses of his mind.

A new breed of killer is stalking the streets of Sam's home city, one so terrifying that everyone, even the usual criminals he deals with, are afraid.

This is no ordinary serial murderer. Sam is hunting the cleverest and most deadly adversary he has ever faced, and as more victims come to light, the killer's gaze settles upon him.

As his personal life is turned upside down, Sam suddenly finds himself the latest plaything of the most horrific murderer he has ever faced.

You better make sure no finds out your dirty little secrets.

www.ingramcontent.com/pod-product-compliance
Lightning Source LLC
Chambersburg PA
CBHW072134170626

46813CB00004BA/1557